THE POISON
TREE

THE POISON TREE

•

Linda Lehmann Masek

AVALON BOOKS
NEW YORK

PRINTED IN THE UNITED STATES OF AMERICA
ON ACID-FREE PAPER
BY HADDON CRAFTSMEN, BLOOMSBURG, PENNSYLVANIA

To my grandparents, Hulda and Jesse
Lehmann, with love always.

And to my baby boy, Checkers.

Prologue

In the beginning . . .
—Genesis, *The Holy Bible*

May, 1718

T he first time Cristabel Lamonte saw Sir Edward Teach, she thought she was madly in love with him. The second time she laid eyes on him, she wanted to run a dagger through his heart. And the third time . . .

Cristabel opened her eyes slowly, confused and unable to remember recent events. Then the events leading up to where she was came seeping back into her mind, like some unwanted nightmare she needed to escape from. There was a gentle rocking movement underneath her. Of course! A ship! He had dragged her off to his flagship, the *Queen Anne's Revenge*, and they had sailed from the Charleston shore. Only the Good Lord above could now be sure of exactly where the ship was heading.

Cristabel raised her head slowly. There was the taste of blood in her mouth; her bruised face peered back at her from the glass on the teak vanity dresser. Her cheek was crusted with dried blood, where Teach had struck her repeatedly after she had tried to resist his advances. Cristabel

Linda Lehmann Masek

lifted herself off the rumpled bed. A torn and dirty quilt fell to the floor as she slowly pulled herself erect.

There was a sick feeling of nausea in the pit of her stomach as she rocked back and forth on the bed slowly; back and forth as she tried to control her thoughts, careening first one way and then another. Cristabel glanced down at the dark red stain on the sheet; blood from the dagger she had tried to plunge into him. The blood had dripped onto her linen petticoats; her blood or his, she could no longer be sure. Edward Teach had dragged her here after literally tearing the clothes half off her body.

Cristabel shuddered in rememberance, smelling again his foul breath and the stench from his unwashed clothes. His black beard had been tangled with saliva, his eyes dark with something that Cristabel instinctively knew was evil. Her frantic cries had gone unanswered, as his elephant-like hands, rough and weatherbeaten, had pushed her savagely into the captain's cabin after they had finally returned to the ship.

Returning to her present terror, the girl shuddered again as she half-pulled, half-dragged herself completely away from the bed. The room swayed for a moment. Cristabel moved toward the teak dresser, searching for a weapon. Suppose he came back. Suppose he tried to take up where he had left off. But she had no weapon. He would hardly be stupid enough to let her get hold of another dagger. No, the room, sparcely furnished, held just the bed and dresser and some sort of clothes press. It seemed as devoid of the opportunity for assistance as the man himself.

How could she have been so deceived about his original intent? When her papa had told them about Teach coming to Woodbridge Plantation, the family had been delighted. Their home in Carolina was in the tidewater region; visitors were not that common. Now here was Papa, telling them of Teach, who had come to protect them. A privateer he had said, who defended the plantation owners from the pirates marauding along the coast. Teach was supposedly a privateer commissioned by Queen Anne of England herself;

one who had sailed under the articles of war. He had come to save them from harm. But instead . . .

Cristabel thought back to the dinner party Papa had held. Edward Teach presented himself at their door, his eyes dark and seeking. His eyes roamed over her; she should have been offended, yet somehow Cristabel was excited, thinking thoughts no proper girl should even be considering about the man across from her at the supper table. Afterward, they had danced to the tunes played by the Negro slave, Jethrow, his fiddle springing to life, his fingers caressing the strings as they danced the country steps her governess had taught them in the schoolroom the previous summer. They had drunk wine, dark red and bubbly. Cristabel had laughed and become dizzy and Edward had asked her if she wanted to go outside.

The moon was veiled in the eastern sky as she had turned and found him very close to her. His hand found her throat as his eyes smoldered, glowing darkly in the torch light of the veranda. Then his hands were tearing at her bodice, dragging her backward off the veranda, slinging her sideways as she tried to scream. She was half-dragged, half-carried like a sack of grain through the heavy underbrush to the coast.

Suddenly, men were around, many men, not garbed in a red satin coat, white shirt, and dark breeches as Edward Teach was. The stench of unwashed bodies invaded her nose as Cristabel was hurled into the longboat these men had beached on the shore. Her head snapped back against the oarlock. She was only dimly conscious of the men as the boat slid back through the silky water to the flagship moored out on the bay.

Cristabel put a hand to her head, the events leading her to the Captain's cabin blurring through the pain. The ship rocked; she could feel the motion through her feet. Her green Moroccan slippers had been knocked off somewhere. As she stood, the room spun like the time she had had too much wine. Her eyes frantically searched the cabin, yet found no weapon of any kind. She knew she had to escape before he returned.

Her bodice had been torn open; she noticed that dark, ugly

welts covered her as Cristabel leaned back once more against the bed. How long had she been here? How long ago had her trust in Teach been shattered when he brought her aboard his ship? It could have been hours or it could have been days. There was no knowing. But someone would be coming soon to rescue her. Of that, Cristabel had no doubt.

And then she heard the footsteps . . .

Cristabel's eyes desperately sought the door, even as her mind told her the tread was far too light to be that of Edward Teach. But who could this be? There was a rapid pulse beating at her throat as she peered anxiously around for her dress to cover herself. It lay on the floor, the shimmering green silk torn and dark with sweat and blood. She yanked it on just as the lock turned in the doorway. The door swung open ominously.

A slight, dark-skinned face peered in; huge, soulful eyes quickly found her. Not Edward Teach, but a mere cabin boy. He slid past the door, carrying a jug of water, some fruit in a basket, and a calabash bowl with fish stew. His clothes were dirty, his trousers torn, and he was barefoot. Cristabel pulled herself farther away onto the bed.

He placed the water and a tin cup on the teak dresser along with the fruit basket. The girl saw the angry welts on his arms and the dark scars around his wrists caused by manacles. He couldn't have been older than her sixteen years, but his eyes seemed ageless as he took in the blood on her clothes and the rumpled bed.

"You eat. Will feel better." He motioned to the fruit. His accent was different from the slaves on the Carolina plantation, more clipped and less sing-song.

Cristabel motioned to him and then to the porthole across from the door. "You are from here? The Carolinas?"

He shook his head. "Barbados."

Then he turned, the whites of his eyes showing, almost frightened as though he had said too much. He eased his way back through the door and was out into the companionway without another word.

Cristabel waited long moments, but heard no other steps. Perhaps Edward Teach had gone; where, she didn't know.

She eased back off the bed and over to the water. Suddenly the girl forgot the taste of blood in her mouth and her torn and filthy clothing. Cristabel was so thirsty that she didn't bother with the tin cup, but began pouring water from the jug down her throat.

Finally, she wiped her mouth with the back of her hand. She knew she had to get out somehow, so she went back to searching the cabin for something to use as a weapon.

Cristabel ran her hands over the teak dresser and pulled open the clothes press. The stale smell of grimy clothes reached her. A pair of Edward Teach's heavy boots lay on the floor, along with two leather coats and some muslin shirts. Cristabel eased the clothes press shut and prowled toward the door, her hands toying with the lock.

And then under her startled gaze, the lock pulled open and back. It had not been securely latched or . . . She thought of the dark sympathy in the eyes of the Negro cabin boy. He had left it deliberately unlatched! But why? And what would happen to him if Teach ever found out?

Her hands were shaking as she pressed her ear to the door. All was silent. The ship rocked back and forth, almost like it was wheezing at its moorings. Cristabel slid the door open, the latch clicking back like bullets from Papa's hunting rifle. A second later and she was in the companionway.

Cristabel slipped silently down the short hall. She wondered where the crew was; handling a ship the size of the *Queen Anne's Revenge* would take many men. The girl shrugged. As long as they weren't skulking around, why worry about them? She pulled open a door at the end of the companionway. Beneath was a short flight of stairs leading to the upper deck.

Then Cristabel saw him; not Teach but a heavily-built man with dirty brown trousers. He was bare chested; his head covered with a red bandana. The man was half-sitting, half-lying close to the rail on the port side of the ship, his bare feet sticking out at an odd angle, his back propped up against some barrels. A tin mug lay at his side along with a pistol and a load of powder.

Cristabel pulled back, but there was no other direction

to go except across the deck. She wrinkled her brow. The man seemed to be alone on the deck. Where were the rest of them? They had to be somewhere close. Edward Teach and his men wouldn't just abandon ship.

A cold sweat coated her body. Perhaps behind her were the rest of the men. But no, the aft part of the ship was empty. The crew was gone, except for the one fellow on the deck and the Negro cabin boy.

Why hadn't he gone too? Cristabel stuck her head back around the corner, her dark hair cascading forward in the wash of the slight wind. She could see the deckhand more clearly now. He pulled a cork out of the nearest barrel and refilled his mug. The pungent odor of rum saturated the deck.

He was intoxicated! The man was supposed to be standing watch, but he was guzzling rum instead! Cristabel leaned back, her hands pressed to her temples. If he was drunk, perhaps it might be possible to crawl over the side and somehow get a boat adrift. Getting *anywhere* would be better than staying on this ship. Anywhere would be safer. And surely Papa and her sister and dear Charles, her betrothed, would be starting to look for her.

Cristabel turned back to the pirate. The fumes from the rum continued to permeate the ship. The man drank deeply from the cup again. The girl heard a hiccup and then his head slowly sagged.

She eased forward. The deck creaked under her weight. She stopped, frozen, like a deer caught in the torch light off the summer kitchen at the plantation. But the fellow snored on. Cristabel placed one bare foot cautiously in front of the other. She had to cross almost in front of him to reach the far rail. Beyond that, she could see the dark shadow of land and some sort of fire blazing.

Another board creaked. The sailor snored on. She kept moving, counting softly to herself; another foot and then another. At last, her outstretched fingers touched the wooden railing. Cristabel pulled herself completely upright and looked over the side.

It was a long way down. Very long. The dark glassy

water reached up from below. And there was no longboat! The bonfire from the land could be seen clearly. There were dark-skinned bodies cavorting in the yellow-flared light. Teach and his men were all on shore! That was where the longboats were. Pulled up on the beach!

A sob rose in Cristabel's throat. There was no way off this ship other than to swim. But could she? Her cousins from Fishport had taught her. Miss Alicia Rogers, Cristabel's governess, had not thought it worthy of a lady and had been furious. But swimming in a quiet forest pool was different from swimming here.

There was a loud snore behind her. She turned, poised to run, but the pirate merely rolled over and went back to sleep, his ragged-trousered legs splayed on the deck.

What choice did she have? The land was close. And if she waited, Edward Teach and his men would be back. Cristabel would never have a better chance than now, when he thought her beaten and unconscious in his cabin.

She dragged herself over to the rail, her fingers searching for any kind of hold. The water below was dark, an inky kind of soulless black. It would be unforgiving if she failed to make it to shore. There would be no tomorrow, here or with Edward Teach, or anywhere.

Cristabel peered back. The pirate on the deck snored on, happily oblivious to anything or anyone. Then her fingers found the rope.

In all probability, it was where the longboat had been tied to the ship. Someone had carelessly left it hanging over the side; or perhaps had been in too much of a hurry to pull it up. Cristabel didn't stop to speculate, but slid over the gunwale and began descending, hand over hand.

The rope burned her fingers as she crawled down. Her arms felt like they were being pulled out of her shoulders. Regardless, she kicked downward in her filthy dress and petticoats. The rope twisted and turned around her like a writhing rattlesnake; it reminded her of the one her betrothed, dear Charles, had killed one day by the back gardens at Woodbridge. He had taken the snake skin and made it into a belt. She could never look at the thing without expressing a shudder, but her Papa had said it was part of the way they lived off of the land and she must get used to things. Cristabel shuddered now as she dropped from the rope and felt the shock of the salt water.

Her dress pulled her down, and at the last second Cristabel untied her petticoats from around her waist and kicked them away. The water washed over her head; she thrashed to the surface, gulped air, and pushed away toward the nearby shore.

It hadn't looked so far from the ship. She swam a few strokes and floated. The current pulled her inward toward land, as she tried not to swallow water. Salt dried her throat and made her skin flame where she had been bruised and battered. She kept going.

Cristabel looked back once at the *Queen Anne's Revenge*. A breeze fanned out over the water, opening the flag that hung from the topmast. It appeared to be a black banner with a figure of what seemed to be a skeleton, shaped like the devil dancing, with a heart and dagger close by. Then the breeze died and the flag went limp. Cristabel trod water for a few moments, hoping devoutly that she would never see the flag or the devil it represented again.

Her nose was filling with water and the heavy material of her dress continued to pull her downward. Gasping, she stared ahead. There was a gigantic bonfire Edward Teach and his men had built on the beach. The black-clad figures moved around it like devils on All Hallow's Eve. Cristabel tried to turn slightly away. She could see the longboats on the shell-covered beach. It wouldn't do for her to splash in too close to the men. If Teach had left a guard, she might be spotted.

The wavelets were quiet and the current strong. She half-floated, half-swam toward the beach beyond their longboats. But it was slow going. She kept spitting out the salt water that washed unbidden down her throat. Finally her stomach rebelled and she started to retch.

Her feet hit the bottom of one of the shoals. Cristabel stood erect, shivering in her wet dress. She eased forward, stepped into a hole on the bottom, and fell flat. Surfacing, she kept to the water, one cautious eye on the beach. She could see Teach and his men close to the bonfire; their torches like gigantic fireflies of light running back and forth in the trees.

What could they be doing? Cristabel skirted the longboats and rose again. The water here was warmer and washed comfortingly around her knees. The heavy skirts she wore made walking almost impossible, while the shells on the beach cut into her bare feet. Regardless, she moved closer, fascinated by the lights from the trees.

"Hurry, lads," Teach's voice boomed out. "Put your backs into it. We must be away on the tide."

Cristabel dropped to the ground and eased herself behind a nearby grass-covered, sandy mound. She could see very well what the men were doing. They were dragging what looked like mahogany chests back among the trees. Six of them. The men strained to lift them, their chest muscles gleaming in the half-light. Beyond, more men were digging what looked to be a gigantic hole. It was far back from the beach, covered by dense shrubbery and some kind of tree that Cristabel had never seen before. She stole forward for a clearer look.

Suddenly Cristabel heard a wracking cough from close to the fire. There was a wheezing sound and she could tell that this fellow wasn't swizzled on rum like the man on the ship.

He was having other problems, too. Cristabel crept closer and watched the pirate tear off, then toss aside leaves and branches from the twenty-foot trees which were found farther back from the beach. His hands turned fiery red with blisters, as a white, milky sap coursed over his fingers. The man swore an oath and rubbed his hands frantically together. This seemed only to increase his agony, as his eyes began watering. Cristabel saw him stagger back and fall over something hard and green that looked like it had tumbled from the branches of the trees. As a sharp pungent odor carried on the slight breeze, she felt her own eyes begin to smart and water, as the girl turned and began crawling back through the underbrush.

Reaching the shelter of the forest, Cristabel rose and peered back for the last time. Teach and his men were returning, trailing back to the beach a few at a time. But the chests of carved mahogany were gone. Teach reached the pirate groaning by the fire and yanked him erect, shoving the man forward. The pirates made a hasty retreat toward the longboats. Cristabel turned and hurried in the opposite direction.

The sharp sand crystals from the beach cut into her feet. Her eyes still stung from the flames, but she dared not stop to find water. Finally, after walking for hours, she sank down into the sand. Her clothes smelled of the salt from the sea and had dried stiff and hard, but at least some of the blood had washed away.

The night was still black while the moon remained an angry slit in the sky. "I'll rest for just a few moments," Cristabel muttered softly to herself. She curled into a ball, bare legs tucked under her shredded green dress. Her petticoats were gone, but the night wind was warm and sultry and she was so tired, her eyes seemed to close by themselves.

"Just for a moment," she murmured again. It was her last conscious thought as her head sagged sideways and she slept.

The dawn was turning the eastern sky to a dark mauve and pink color when Cristabel awoke. White egrets with long bills were skimming over the water. Cristabel raised her head, her long dark hair falling forward. Her lips were parched and cracked from the lack of water. She had to get a drink from somewhere.

Slinking back from the ocean, the girl moved up the coast and into the fields of sea oats. Orange-red flowers trailed around her bare legs. There had to be fresh water here somewhere. But where was *here?* Was she still on the shore or out on one of the Carolina isles? Cristabel looked down the beach. It stretched as far as she could see; rocky sand mixed with the sparse, willowy grasses. The brown pelicans were diving for fish out on the water. If only she were a bird, Cristabel thought idly, all of her troubles would be solved.

She wandered inland, out of the sun and through the

cooler underbrush. The sky was obscured by the overhead branches of oak and hickory trees. Cristabel sank down as her head began to swim with dizziness. She could not go much farther without help.

Then she saw the birds rise in a shimmering white cloud ahead of her. What had frightened them? The breeze increased from across the water. Cristabel hesitated and dragged herself behind a nearby rock. She would wait and see what came down the path in front of her. Perhaps it was nothing; an animal could be on the prowl. Surely Edward Teach and his crew had left with the tide. They were probably long gone by now. Even as the thought crossed her mind, her skin broke out in clammy sweat. Suppose they hadn't left. Suppose he was looking for her right now.

Cristabel looked back and gasped aloud in despair. Her bare feet had made tracks through the soft earth of the forest. She could see the footprints even as she saw the tall sea grasses hovering back and forth. Someone was coming! She could feel his presence as if he had called her by name!

Cristabel stood erect. The forest and beach and water all swam together before her gaze. The thought came to her that she was too weak and tired to go any farther. The men from the ship would have no trouble catching her now. She was too sick to resist.

The girl sank back and curled herself once more into a small, miserable ball, her head bowed under her arms. Perhaps if she stayed very quiet, they would just walk on past. She stayed still, barely able to breath. Peering out between her fingers, she saw ragged, brown trouser legs come into view. The legs stopped, obviously following her very plain trail. He continued, paused, then moved beside the grass. Cristabel looked up, drawn by a force she didn't understand. A hand reached down to her, a brown hand with a wrist scarred from the manacles of many chains. Slave chains. Fresh blood from whip cuts on his arms, up and down, made a savage, grotesque pattern.

She gasped and raised her eyes to his face. Sympathetic, soul-searching black eyes looked down at her. A long moment passed. Then she placed her hand in his and smiled.

Chapter One

The smallest feline is a masterpiece.
—Leonardo Da Vinci

May, 2002

Josephine Sharpe officially lost her husband and found her cat on one and the same day, thereby linking these two dissimilar events together in her mind for all eternity. The husband, whose name was Glen Howard, was notified of Josephine's desire for a divorce as quickly and painlessly as possible. A signature on the dotted line was all that was required, and their five-year union would be dissolved forever. The story of the cat, however, was a bit more complicated.

Josephine looked at slanty, hazel eyes through the kitty cage; soulful eyes that somehow managed to appear helpless yet independent all at the same time. A tiger body along with a mangled right ear completed the picture.

Jo turned from the cat cage to face the gimlet-blurred eyes of a woman across the room.

"But nobody said anything about an animal when you called my bookstore about your late mother's effects."

This was certainly the truth, Jo thought to herself. Bridie MacPherson's daughter had merely said that her mother had left two trunks of "odds and ends", and since she was trying to tidy-up the house so it could be sold, she needed Jo to come to the Island and collect the trunks.

"Well, I'm saying it now." Lorna Glutt pursed her small painted mouth and wrinkled her nose as though she smelled something sour in the room. Whether it was Jo or the cat was hard to say.

"If you really don't want the beast, I suppose I'll have to take him over to the animal shelter. There's one in Manteo somewhere."

Jo nodded absentmindedly. Roanoke Island was an independent community all on its own, connected by causeway to the Outer Banks and Nag's Head, where her bookshop, Learned Owls, was to be found. She really couldn't be expected to take Bridie's cat home. At least she didn't think so. As Lorna moved with a determined, mannish stride toward the carrier, Jo saw the animal shrink back. Its eyes turned once more toward her. Jo thought she would never forgive herself if she ignored the look in those limpid, black pools.

"All right. I'll take him." Jo shoved her short, dark hair back from her forehead. "Perhaps I could use a new friend, now that my divorce is being finalized."

Lorna Glutt sniffed. "Well, nobody thought that marriage of yours had much of a chance. Fancy, rich, New York publisher. What could he possibly see in someone like you?"

Jo glared at the other woman. Was she being deliberately cruel or just dense? Lorna stared back at her, a stony expression on her face. No wonder her mother had wanted to live alone out on Roanoke Island! Lorna would be enough to bust anyone's bubble! Although, in all fairness, she was possibly just repeating the local gossip.

"Glen wasn't always from New York, although that was where we met. He originally came from down this way, too. From Ocracoke Island."

"Right down the causeway a piece." Lorna Glutt nodded sagely, her dyed red hair flopping forward. "I heard he was one of the Howards from Howard Street. That was years ago, of course. He got off the island, moved to New York, and made a pot of money."

"Pots of money. And you heard right. At any rate," Jo turned to the cat, "I'll take Kitty home. I hope he likes living in an apartment over the bookstore."

"Bound to like it better than the pound." Lorna Glutt followed Jo out to her black Chevy. She watched as the other woman loaded the cat carrier plus the small trunks into the back of the car.

Jo straightened and wiped her hands on her cutoff jeans. She turned back to Lorna.

"So do you have any prospects for this old place." Jo looked at the house. The stone front and white latticework badly needed paint, but the old Victorian had character written all over it. A turreted room occupied one front side, while the wide front porch looked out over what once had been a beautiful English garden.

Lorna snorted. "This monstrosity? Never. I tried and tried to get Mother to move into town with me and sell this white elephant. Now it's literally falling down. But the land is worth something of course. And it's close enough to Manteo and the Sound. I had such a nice little attic apartment fixed up for Mother. But she just wouldn't consider it."

"Can't imagine why," Jo muttered under her breath to the cat. She tossed her baggy, cloth purse into the car and climbed in.

"All the best." Lorna sucked on a tooth. "If you hear of any hot-shot movie star who is looking for property, tell him to give me a call. You never know. Andy Griffith settled here. Maybe somebody with loot will come along. Maybe even that Howard fellow you were hitched up with."

"Er, right." *Heaven help me. I may shoot her yet!* Jo put the car into gear, forcing Lorna to step back or have her toes run over.

"Oh, by the way, what's his name?" She nodded at the cat.

Lorna Glutt looked like she had never heard such an inane question in her life. "Why, Cat, of course. What else?"

"What else, indeed," Jo mumbled as she backed cautiously out of the rutted, unkempt driveway and down Mother Vineyard Road, leading through the center of Manteo to the causeway. Lorna Glutt waved dutifully before turning back to plant a large "For Sale" sign in front of the old Victorian. Then the vision was lost in the heavy underbrush of Roanoke Island.

Traffic was heavy as Jo maneuvered the Chevy around one pothole after another. Finally, she swung left on the Nag's Head–Manteo Causeway and breathed a sigh of relief.

"I don't know about you, Kitty, but I'm glad to get out of there. It can only get better!"

The cat stared back at her as though in agreement that Lorna Glutt was indeed a piece of work.

Jo glanced right at the solid stream of traffic heading toward the Elizabethan Gardens and the North Carolina Aquarium on Roanoke Island and shook her head. The line of cars was incredible, in part due to the azure sky overhead without a cloud to mar the scene.

"The tourists seem to be out in full force, Kitty. All the more reason to get back to my bookstore. We may actually make some money this afternoon."

The cat remained silent as Jo angled her way along Route 64. Cruising past Sir Walter Raleigh Street, another line of cars waiting to get into the Festival Park Marina and the History Center met her gaze. Jeanine's Cat House, one of her favorite shops, was also overrun with visitors. Normally the town of Manteo had a little over fifteen hundred residents, but with the influx of tourists, there were possibly ten times that number looking at antiques and local handicrafts, and attending the island's theater.

Jo exhaled again as she reached the causeway crossing from the island to Nag's Head. The salty sea air blew her dark hair in a cloud around her elfin face. Passing the Weeping Radish Restaurant and Brewery and the Windmill Pond Restaurant, she noted that Charlie's Dolphin Tour boats were out in the sound searching for their elusive prey on the flat, bluish-gray water. As Jo looked toward home, she spotted the gigantic sand dunes of Jockey's Ridge State Park, where the Wright Brothers had made their famous airplane flight almost a hundred years before. The golden promontory of land stuck out like a pointing finger across the water. Jo knew that years earlier in the eighteenth century, "bankers" had lured ships into the shore using lanterns tied onto pack animals. Ship captains, assuming these hanging lights were other vessels, would run aground and end up being robbed by the locals, their entire cargo being pillaged.

Jo swung the car past the sandy dunes and innumerable vacation homes, standing three and four stories high on stilts, like some science fiction houses. The stilts protected homes from the frequent high water on the Atlantic side of Nag's Head. As Jo pulled into the Learned Owls Bookshop, sandwiched between the Ramada Inn on one side and a three-story vacation home half-completed on the other, the picture was complete.

Tara Cataldo's bright yellow Volkswagen, decorated with orange sunflowers, was parked out front. Aside from that, the parking lot was empty.

"Come on, Kitty. Time to check out your new home." Jo grasped the carrier and eased inside. The cool air conditioning was a relief from the heat of the unusually warm day.

Tara Cataldo, her black-haired college student assistant, was sitting behind the cash register wearing a T-shirt with the slogan "Life Sucks" across the front and dark blue shorts. She simultaneously looked up from the mystery book she was reading while shoving her glasses up toward her khaki-brown eyes.

"Jo! You're back already! And you missed all of our customers!" Tara turned the book she had been reading face down on the counter next to the old-fashioned cash register.

Jo set the cat carrier on the floor and glanced curiously at the book.

"Don't tell me you read over three hundred pages of

Phillip Marlowe playing detective in *The Big Sleep* since I left. It isn't possible!"

Tara grinned, showing a cracked front tooth along with braces. "Not a chance. I always read the endings first. That's what I'm doing now."

"But what's the point? There's no surprise if you know how it ends, is there?"

"But that is the point! I like happy endings! If I don't like the way it ends, why should I bother reading over three hundred pages? No happy ending, no read!"

"I see. At least, I think I see."

At that moment, Kitty let out a plantitive meow. Tara hopped off her stool and bent to investigate.

"Now who is this?" She stuck an inquiring finger into the cage. Kitty promptly licked her finger.

"Bridie MacPherson's cat. I inherited him when I went to collect the boxes of old books." Jo dropped her purse on one of the two overstuffed chairs in the reading area of the bookstore. "He had a one-way ticket to the animal shelter." She stared into the tiger cat's deep eyes. "I told her I'd give him a home."

Tara opened the carrier. Kitty immediately climbed out and settled on a stool by the cash register.

"I'm glad you did! See, he's at home already!"

Jo collapsed into a chair. Her gaze moved down past the children's section, with its stuffed animal toys, back to the adult fiction and mysteries. The small storage room in the back of the store was where she did the book mending and kept antique volumes. A spiral staircase led from this room to her apartment on the second floor.

"So did anyone call while I was gone?"

Tara stopped rubbing Kitty's head and moved to the telephone pad.

"Yes. Your friend, Cyn Savene. Asked you to call her back in New York. Wanted to know how you were doing. Also, a Mr. Glen Howard. He asked for Josephine Sharpe."

Tara pushed her glasses farther up toward her eyes. "I didn't know your first name was Josephine. And Glen Howard, that sounds familiar."

"I'm sure that wasn't the message," Jo said wryly. "And yes, Josephine is my real name. And please, no wisecracks about the song. "Oh, come Josephine in my flying machine . . .' That joke got rather lame years ago."

"It wasn't what I was thinking. The only Josephine I've heard of is Josephine Tey, the author. She wrote *Brat Farrar*. A great story."

"You've read it?"

"Not exactly. I saw the PBS movie a while back. But I would have read it if I had thought of it! Actually, I meant to read it!"

"You doth object too much," Jo said, paraphrasing Shakespeare. "Anyway what else did Mr. Howard say? Aside from coming out with my full name?"

"Something about not signing some papers. He wants to talk to you first."

Tara closed the telephone pad with a click. She looked expectantly at Jo like a tiny hummingbird looking for a handout.

"All right. I might as well tell you the story. Glen Howard is my soon-to-be ex-husband. As soon as he signs the divorce papers my attorney sent him last month. He's probably in New York—which is where I was—working as an editor. He and I met at a literary luncheon and one thing led to another and we ended up getting married." Jo's mouth twisted bitterly. "It was a mistake from day one."

"But why is his name so familiar to me? Is he a writer?"

"No. A publisher. He publishes *Alive!* magazine among other things. Glen made his money sponsoring authors who later became extremely successful. He has a Midas touch for making money. I just wish it had carried over to our personal relationship."

Tara snapped her fingers. "Ho-Jo Publications. Howard and Josephine?" She looked pointedly at Jo.

"Right. He named it after me. In happier times, of course."

Tara's eyes widened. "He named an entire publishing house after you? And now he won't sign the divorce papers? He must really want to get back together!"

"I don't! And this is one time," Jo said with determination, "that Mr. Howard is not going to get what he wants, which is me back as his loving wife in New York!"

"Howard . . . He's not from around here, is he?"

"Right you are. Fresh off of Ocracoke Island, believe it or not." Jo reached over to scratch the kitty behind his ears. "It's strange, Glen coming from there. He wanted to get out, go elsewhere, do something. We met in New York, of all places. And I'm the one who ends up back here, buying this bookstore from one of the locals, when I wasn't the one who wanted to get away!"

"Local? Which local? You forget I'm not from this area but farther south. From around Beaufort."

"From Possum Slocum. He wanted to retire and paint landscapes full time. So he sold me the Learned Owls. Now he sells paintings to the tourists over on Manteo. He's not a bad artist," Jo added as an afterthought.

"But there's no money in that," Tara interrupted. "I've never known a painter to hit it big until after he died. And then, what good does it do them?"

"At any rate, I'm going to be unavailable to take Mr. Howard's calls. Sooner or later he'll accept the inevitable, sign those damn papers and we can both get on with our lives."

Tara looked curious. "He sounded so nice. Was it . . . another woman who caused the breakup?"

"No. Much worse. I could have dealt with female competition. No," Jo said sadly, "it was work. Work and more work. Glen wanted to make it big as a publisher. It was the number one dream on his list. And I don't think I figured on the list at all. Me or the family I wanted to have."

Jo rose abruptly from the chair where she had been sitting. "I think I see an actual customer pulling in. Why don't you check and find out what she wants while I take Bridie MacPherson's boxes out of my car. Who knows, there really might be something of value in there."

"Sure." Tara paused, looking at Kitty. "You know, I've had a thought. About a name." She indicated the Raymond

Chandler book she had been reading. "What about Marlowe for our little tiger friend? Do you like it?"

"Marlowe." Jo tasted the name on her lips. "Why not? I always was a Humphrey Bogart fan. He'll be the official cat of the Learned Owls."

Tara snuggled up against Marlowe's neck. "I'm so glad we're keeping him. Welcome, Marlowe," she murmured softly, her lips curving into a delighted smile.

Chapter Two

Her gentle limbs did she undress,
And lay down in her loveliness.
—Samuel Taylor Coleridge, *Cristabel*

It was later that same day, after Jo had eaten her Lean Cuisine and Marlowe had guzzled chicken bits, that she finally looked at the trunks from Bridie MacPherson's home. Tara had left shortly after 6:00, promising to bring yummies for Marlowe the next day. She had helped Jo drag the small-sized trunks up the outside staircase and through the screened porch to Jo's apartment above the bookstore. Now Jo was rummaging happily through Bridie's effects, supervised by Marlowe, who had adopted a beige armchair as his own.

Jo collected a pile of picture albums, notebooks, and papers, and dragged everything over to the desk next to the fireplace in her main room. From there, she could look out across the porch on a field of reddish-brown gaillardia to the beach and the ocean beyond. The sky was a deep cerulean shade, crossed by marble streaks of whitish cloud. The sun was perhaps three-quarters of the way into its bed for the night. The waves were quiet with tiny, spotted rivulets washing sporadically up onto the grainy beach. It was so peaceful, so still. Ideal for soul-searching, Jo thought grimly. She just wasn't sure she had enough energy to really search. The problem was that Tara had opened her Pandora's Box with questions, and Jo was unable to just close it with a bang as she would have liked.

There were several things regarding her marriage to Glen Howard that she hadn't mentioned to Tara, including the real reason she had come to North Carolina after being born and bred in New York. Glen had brought her down years earlier to meet his family on Ocracoke Island. She had found the area enchanting and almost mesmerizing with its open expanses of beach and wild ponies that roamed at will, and shoals where pirates once evaded capture from the authorities. The tall, stately lighthouse, standing like a white sentinel on the shore, guarded the village beyond. For a city girl, the wide-open spaces of the dunes and the salt sea beyond had provided a freedom from her tight, confined existence in the city.

Glen's reaction to the place had been exactly the opposite. Where she had found freedom, he had found boredom. After confiding to her that he hated the island, he had described it as a sun-filled pit, where a bunch of has-been artists, writers, or whatever lolled away their time because they weren't good enough or bright enough to cut it in the real world. His summation complete, they had left Ocracoke and flown to Paris for their honeymoon. While she looked at Chanel gowns and Joy perfume, Glen had set up a Paris branch of Ho-Jo Publications.

Jo had never forgotten the Outer Banks and when she was searching for a place to open her bookstore, she had remembered the rejuvenating sea and sky that had brought her happiness—happiness before everything had gone indescribably sour.

"No, Glen won't be back here in a hurry, Marlowe," Jo spoke aloud to the cat. "His business couldn't survive the separation."

Marlowe purred loudly and rolled over on his back, tiger feet waving in the air. Jo laughed before attacking the second trunk that Lorna Glutt had given her that morning.

Bridie MacPherson had collected odds and ends like a pack rat. Jo found an old album with wedding pictures from the turn of the century, the pictures brown and yellow with age. Bridie's mother perhaps, or even grandmother? There were some pictures of Bridie and a tall, rather handsome man with a dark mustache in an army uniform. A pilot in the war from what Jo could see of the insignia. And there were pictures of a sullen, dark-haired little girl—could this possibly be Lorna?—with Band-Aids all over her knobby knees.

Jo sighed, stretched, and closed the volume with a snap. She moved out onto the screened stucco porch and looked below to the bookstore. The place was quiet now; the nearby Oregon Inlet Road, which led back to Whalebone Junction and the causeway, was finally deserted of traffic. Lights in the Ramada Inn blinked on and off like beacons next door to her apartment; a group of people were having a party out on one of the balconies. Farther down the dark expanse of beach, she could see the lights from the pier reaching out into the blackness. A saxophone played in the Barracuda Bar, its mellow tones whispering in the distance.

Jo swatted at one of the overlarge North Carolina mosquitoes that had smuggled itself in on the screened porch. She turned and wandered back inside to rummage once again in the larger of the two trunks. A whole life full of memories. In two trunks. Jo wondered for a moment if it was how she would end up. But no, Glen was behind her, along with their unborn child. A child that she dared not even now think about.

"Not everyone is like Glen," she spoke aloud firmly. "All men aren't the same."

It was just a matter of finding one that had more common ground with her, and less quicksand. Glen Howard had been the quicksand. Once the divorce was behind her, she could return to solid ground and all would be well.

She yanked at the last trunk impatiently, suddenly wishing Bridie and her daughter well behind her. The trunk sagged inward and a brown, leather-bound volume slipped out and onto the floor. Jo bent over and picked it up. The leather was well-worn as though the book had been opened many, many times. She turned the flyleaf over and read the inscription, written in a flowery, dramatic hand with quill pen and ink.

Diarie of Cristabel Ann Marie de Lamonte in the years of Our Lord, 1715 to 1718.

Jo peeked ahead, curious as to what a young girl living at the time North Carolina had first been settled would have to talk about. The diary seemed authentic, at least as far as Jo could tell. The writer blotted her ink at intervals, a rather blue-black color, now faded. The writing was on brownish parchment—yellow, stiff, and partially blackened with age.

Cristabel would have lived in Carolina prior to the Revolutionary War, shortly after the area was settled. Jo knew a little about American History, but nothing all that specific about the Carolinas. She flicked on an overhead light, squinted at the vellum, and started to read.

My name is Cristabel and I have received this diarie as a gift from my beloved papa on my thirteenth birthday. I have taken it upon myself to record major events from my life here on our plantation in the Carolinas, along with those of my family—Papa, my sister, Rose-Clare, and my brother Robert. My mother, alas, passed away when my younger sister Rose-Clare was born ten years ago. So now there are just the four of us: my uncle, William, who lives in Fishport and my governess, Mistress Alicia Rogers, plus the Negro slaves on the plantation. Mistress Rogers has remonstrated with me about keeping this diarie but feels that it will improve my penmanship, a necessary skill for young ladies living in these times.

Jo smiled. Cristabel sounded so young, so innocent. She flicked through a number of pages. Cristabel spent most of her time in the schoolroom, learning penmanship, sewing, French, and "how to manage a household of her own." Jo read about Cristabel's interest in the cotton and indigo her father grew and the trips down the river to Fishport, where they sold their crops. She spoke of stitching her own clothes—silk and satin with bodices trimmed with ribbon, and long skirts which dragged in the oppressive summer heat. Hats were common to protect fair skin from the sun and sea wind, as were gloves to protect the hands from blisters and callouses not befitting a lady.

Mistress Rogers tutored the sisters in French—the language of culture in their world—and taught her charges to play the pianoforte.

Jo flicked through the diary. Cristabel's life seemed quiet enough until the spring of the following year. Her brother came down with some "mysterious fever" causing discoloration of the skin and night sweats, which eventually caused him to just waste away. Her papa had treated him with medicines from his chest of drugs, but to no avail. Robert passed away a month later amid mourning by all on the plantation. He was buried in the family cemetery not far from the main house, surrounded by "pink starfire trees which bloom in the spring."

Jo jumped ahead again. The family seemed to have finally settled down once more. Cristabel's papa seemed to have become seriously interested in his daughter's governess. This made sense, since his son and heir had passed away and girls normally did not inherit property in those days.

Cristabel recorded her father's marriage the following year. The two girls wore white summer dresses trimmed with French lace, with fashionable three-quarter length sleeves and long ribbons decorating the full skirts.

Jo rubbed her eyes wearily. It had to be after midnight, yet she found the diary fascinating. The following section was even more so as Cristabel continued.

Today I have met the man I am going to marry! His name is Charles Townsend from the neighboring plantation of Oakridge. He rode over and found me picking camellias in our garden for my brother's grave. Dearest Robert has been dead now these past months and Charles was ever so understanding. He went with me

to the family plot and we prayed together for dear
Robert's soul to fly straight to Our Lord in heaven.
And he, I scarcely dare say it, was so excited, took
one of the camillias and wound it into my hair! His
touch was as soft as the petals falling from the roses
in the spring rain. And tomorrow we will be riding
out together with my new stepmama to keep us com-
pany. I am so thrilled! I just know I will not be able
to sleep tonight! Will the morning never come?

As Jo turned the page, she found a withered dried flower
pressed into the page of the diary. Had the young Charles
given this flower to Cristabel? And had it remained pressed
in the volume for all these years? As Jo touched the leaves,
the petals crumbled, its brittleness apparent. Had Cristabel
loved him so much then? Perhaps as only a fifteen-year-
old can, Jo thought sadly.

Jo skipped ahead again over the next dozen pages. Cristabel spoke of visitors to the plantation, neighbors, and also
a "pyrate named Major Bonnet", who visited in March. She
spoke of her beloved papa showing the visitors around the
fields of indigo and rice and of the medicines cultivated in
her new mama's herb garden.

Cristabel's family stayed on the plantation, not far from
the coast, during the humid summer months and when disease was running riot in the young Carolina colony. In winter, they traveled south to Fishport, where there were more
planters and more of an intermingling of society. Here
"dear Papa" sold his crops of rice and indigo and purchased
slaves on the auction block to work the fields back home.

Their townhouse in Fishport was "made of red brick"
with a large summer kitchen, and was where the family
took up residence in the winter months. Jo smiled upon
reading of Cristabel's impressions.

This vile mud in Fishport where Papa does his busi-
ness; I detest it! I detest it even more! My skirts are
drenched everyday when we go out for our daily walk!
And I miss my dear Charles. My soul pines daily for

*him, as I wonder what he is doing, or saying, or where
he is riding out to. The parties here are nice but nothing can replace Charles in my affection. I count the
days, nay the hours, until I can see him again! Do I
sound besotted, dearest Diarie. Well, I am and am not
ashamed to admit it!*

The pages skimmed by. Then in May of 1718, after the
family had made the sojourn to the north, an event happened that changed Cristabel's life forever.

Jo's eyes narrowed. Evidently George Lamonte, Cristabel's papa, invited some "gentlemen" to his home, one Edward Teach plus a number of his cohorts. Teach, according
to Cristabel, had been a privateer, commissioned by the
Queen of England herself. After the war had ended, Edward
Teach had turned pirate, but was pardoned for his sins by
the governor of North Carolina. Evidently, due to this par-
don, Teach had been invited to George Lamonte's plantation home, not far from the Carolina inland waterways.

Cristabel had written of being "enchanted" with the
darkly attractive Teach, with his barrel chest and forbidding
yet somehow exciting appearance. The young ladies tittered
and half-swooned behind their Chinese sandlewood fans.
Teach went out of his way to ingratiate himself over supper. Having selected his prey, the man asked a flattered
Cristabel to walk with him on the magnolia-strewn path-
ways, only to throw the girl over his shoulder and escape
with his hostage to the safety of his ship.

Jo was now wide awake, as Cristabel recorded her terror
aboard ship. After the *Queen Anne's Revenge* had left port,
the girl told of lapsing into unconsciousness then awaking
when the ship docked. After escaping with the help of the
slave boy who had been left to look after her, Cristabel
swam to the shore. There she saw the pirates dragging six
chests of treasure off into the woods. And finally Cristabel
spoke of the tree "with a vile smell when burned, that
caused eyes to water and skin to blister—a poison tree" on
the nearby shore, where she had dragged herself.

"Treasure," Jo muttered aloud. But where had the pirates

been? Directly north from Fishport were the Carolina isles, specifically Ocracoke, where Edward Teach, alias Black-beard, had his pirate's den. Had he buried the treasure on Ocracoke?

Jo read on.

After running away from the campfire and the "poison trees," Cristabel seemed to have wandered around, finally collapsing in exhaustion. One of the last entries in the diary told of finding a white, sandy beach covered with "balloon-type fish with stingers" floating in the water.

These could be Portuguese man-o'-war, Jo thought idly. But it wasn't much of a clue as to where the girl was. The last entry told of Cristabel being followed and running ter-rified away from the coast into the nearby brush. She was found by the cabin boy, his arms covered with bruises and blood where he had been beaten, probably by Blackbeard when the pirate had discovered the girl was gone. Evidently the boy had escaped shortly after the pirates had sailed and followed the girl into the woods.

Had he been a friend or foe? And had Cristabel ever seen him again? Jo asked the questions to herself. Certainly Cristabel had escaped and written the diary sometime later.

Jo turned over the final leaf of the diary. There was one entry on the last page, made later, in a different color ink, but still a woman's hand.

The words burned into Jo's heart and made her mourn for the young Cristabel Lamonte, who would never be young again.

Sometimes I wish he would have slain me. They are all devils—t'is no other word. May the Good Lord forgive me my sins, but it would have been better if I had perished there than to have lived on in this man-ner.

Chapter Three

But whispering tongues can poison truth.
—Coleridge, *Cristabel*

"What do you know about poison trees?" Jo Sharpe asked her bookstore assistant, Tara Cataldo, the next morning. "And a town called Fishport in Carolina history?"

Tara shoved her glasses back on her nose and straightened. She had been hand-feeding Marlowe cat treats, much to the latter's delight. Jo had wandered down the spiral staircase from her upstairs apartment a few moments earlier before the Learned Owls was supposed to open.

"Well, Fishport is easy. It was the name for Beaufort, just south of here. It's where a lot of the big plantation owners stocked up on slaves every so often since they needed them to work the fields back home." Tara eased herself into a chair behind the cash register. She was wearing a dark-blue T-shirt with the motto "I'd rather be scuba-diving." The usual cutoff jeans and sandals completed the ensemble. She had also recently manicured her nails; the blood-red polish reminded Jo of an eagle's talons closing around some unfortunate prey.

"And the poison tree? Have you ever heard of anything like that around here?" Jo eased her lanky frame into one of the oversized, comfortable chairs and propped her feet up on the coffee table.

"Poison tree? No, the only poison tree I know of is a poem written by William Blake that we had to memorize back in my English literature class. Here, take a look." Tara hopped over to the far aisle of the store and pulled a volume from the non-fiction shelves. "This one should have it," she mumbled. "Although I personally like Blake's 'Tyger tyger' much better."

Jo took the extended volume and scanned the poem. "I don't see any connection," she said as she shut the book with a snap.

"Why all the interest in trees and such? Have you taken up horticulture?"

"No. I found this diary in Bridie MacPherson's effects. I can't imagine where it came from." She described to Tara in a few sentences what she had learned of Cristabel Lamonte and her fate at the hands of the pirates.

Tara frowned. "So this girl was kidnapped and er . . . assaulted by Blackbeard? That's interesting since I heard he had a number of wives. Didn't seem to have much trouble getting the fairer sex to fall in love with him either."

"The part about the treasure is strange, though. Cristabel talks about six chests of treasure. Could they have buried it down by Fishport, or on one of the islands, perhaps?"

"There's an estuary right out in the bay by Fishport. Er . . . Beaufort. Right now it's a wildlife refuge. For wild ponies and birds and such. It was dedicated to Rachel Carson. You know, the author of *Silent Spring*."

"Perhaps the *Queen Anne's Revenge* was there then?"

"Oh, it's there all right. Permanently," Tara Cataldo added abruptly.

Jo raised an eyebrow and reached out as Marlowe jumped up onto her chair and settled in her lap.

"You haven't been following the newspapers. A company called Scisearch found the remains of a 16th-century vessel outside of Beaufort Harbor. The ship had been sunk after running aground on the shoals. Anyway," here Tara lowered her voice dramatically, "they think it is the *Queen Anne's Revenge!*"

"Blackbeard's flagship," Jo said slowly. "So he definitely

would know his way around those islands. How is it that you've heard so much?"

Tara pointed to her T-shirt. "I've been diving there. Scisearch came out to the college a few months back. It seems they were interested in people with computer backgrounds who could scuba. It was all very hush-hush. But what they needed were local people who were interested in helping salvage the ship!"

"So you've been diving the *Queen Anne's Revenge?* Tell me, are they still looking for people to help out?"

Tara grinned. "Always. And I seem to remember seeing a mask and fins up in your apartment." She leaned backward on her chair too far and almost slid off in her excitement. "You could call them up. We could go down to Fishport—I mean Beaufort—this next weekend!"

"Wait, not so fast. I haven't been underwater in a long time!"

"Oh, heck!" Tara turned as a bell dinged and a heavyset woman dragging a small boy in her wake came through the door. "It's like swimming or riding a bicycle. You never forget!"

Jo had returned to her office, accompanied by Marlowe, to pay bills and field telephone calls. Tara waited on three customers in a row. Saturday was frequently a busy morning in the Learned Owls bookstore. It was as though people were stocking up on reading material for the rest of the week.

Jo stared out the window toward Oregon Inlet Road. She saw a group of white ibis from the bird sanctuary lift upward, sounding like a group of hysterical children laughing. Beyond the birds and the Ramada Inn was Whalebone Junction, where the Virginia Dare Causeway ran over to Manteo Island. It was also where Route 12 joined in, going south past the the Cape Hatteras Lighthouse and National Seashore to the end of the island where a ferryboat connected to Ocracoke Island. Ocracoke, referred to as Blackbeard's Haven, housed a historic hotel, a "hole" where Blackbeard made his headquarters. Countless other references to the pirate king abounded on the island. Although the Ocracoke locals disdained the hype, many made use of it as a tourist attraction of the highest order. Jo remembered endless comments about the pirates when she and her soon-to-be ex-husband, Glen, had visited down there.

Jo recollected trailing through the the town on a stifling hot day, Glen at her side, peering at the stark, white light-house, the oldest one still working in the country, as the local assistant at the Blackbeard's Inn was proud to tell. The heat had been oppressive and everyone had taken to the air con-ditioned shops and attractions. One of those attractions, lo-cated near "Blackbeard's Hole," had been a museum.

Jo turned to her computer and logged into the website "Switchboard." There was a number listed for the Black-beard Museum on Ocracoke. It was now after ten o'clock on Saturday. Surely someone should be there.

Someone was. The voice that picked up the telephone sounded young, breathless, and identified herself as a vol-unteer. She spoke with the nasal twang of a New Englan-der. Probably a transplant from up north, Jo thought, just like she was herself.

Jo related the facts: old diary, mentioned Blackbeard, could be authentic, and was there anyone she could talk to about it?

There was a pause at the other end. The nasal twang continued.

"Where are you located? There is an expert, local natu-rally, who knows everything that is worth knowing about Blackbeard. Maybe you could give him a call. He just came back from a trip to New York. He's been publicizing his new book on the subject, *Pirates of the Caribbean Area.* I think Blackbeard rates a couple of chapters at least."

Jo frowned. She didn't fancy a drive down to Ocracoke. Aside from her personal reasons for avoiding the place, the ferry lines on a Saturday would be backed up for hours. She vaguely remembered Glen ranting about the locals who never learned how to take reservations, and why didn't they build a bridge to the mainland like sane, normal people? Jo had retorted that perhaps the local people liked the peace and quiet and maybe they didn't want a bridge and the commercialization that would go with it. Glen had merely snorted his disdain for "people not liking inevitable progress in the world."

The girl with the nasal twang cleared her throat. Jo realized she had been silent a long time.

"I'm over on Nag's Head, around the corner from the causeway at Whalebone Junction. The Learned Owls bookstore."

"Oh, there's no problem then. Norm is over at the Aquarium and Research Facility just north of you at Currituck. It's not far. Right by the lighthouse. Just follow Route 158. You should have no trouble."

"I'm familiar with the area. You said Norm?"

"Yes. Norman Switec. He's a writer, librarian, and teacher at the research facility. Does lectures out there on fish native to these waters. He's also a consultant on some dive site down in Beaufort. I don't know that much about it. Supposed to be very secretive and they didn't tell me a thing."

I can't imagine why, Jo thought to herself. The woman was as bad as a town crier. Then she felt a pang of guilt. The girl was probably just trying to be friendly, which seemed to be a trait on the Outer Banks. Jo's citified New York ways were always creeping in.

"So do I need an appointment or anything?" Jo murmured casually.

Nasal Twang laughed. "No, of course not. Norm will be at the aquarium lecturing about underwater discoveries in the area. And the pirates, naturally."

Naturally. "Great. I'll just stop in, then. Thanks for your help."

Jo replaced the telephone and turned back to her computer. She typed in the name Norman Switec in the blank box of her favorite search engine. The computer's spiders coughed up a list of a dozen items about the man, including a book site for *Pirates of the Caribbean Area.*

So he was authentic. Jo could take the diary along, stash it in the car, and see how the interview went. But suddenly she felt a reluctance to show Cristabel Lamonte's most private thoughts to just anyone, especially somebody who might end up writing about the young girl at a future time. She certainly did want to talk to this Blackbeard expert to see if the time lines matched up and to find out if Blackbeard was really the one who had kidnapped young Cristabel and so changed her life.

The telephone shrilled as Jo logged off her computer. She paused, undecided. The last person she wanted to talk to was her soon-to-be ex-husband, Glen. Although he was more likely head-over-ears in work at his office in New York. Even on a Saturday, *Alive!* magazine deadlines had to be met, regardless of the weekend break.

Jo grasped the phone and breathed a sigh of relief at the woman's voice which came over the line.

"Hi, stranger. I was beginning to think we'd never connect." Cyn Savene's voice came through loud and clear.

Jo breathed easier. Cyn had been her sole supporter during the time of her pregnancy and the loss of her baby two years ago. She always had had words of encouragement for her older girlfriend. And, Jo hoped, vice-versa.

"I'm glad to hear from you. How are things going with your new husband?" Jo had attended Cyn's fourth wedding six months earlier, but her friend had become extremely morose and quiet since then.

Cyn laughed. "How did it go in *My Fair Lady?* 'It was doomed from the time she took the vow.' Although any man that couldn't remember not to call me Cindy . . ." Jo smiled. She could almost see in her mind Cyn shudder at the other end of the line. "That *Cindy* made me feel like a charwoman in a Victorian novel."

"So you're unattached again." Jo searched frantically for Number Four's name. Randy? Or was it Ralph?

"Rusty and I just didn't have that much in common. We did both like to spend money, though."

"So how much is this one going to cost your family?"

"I haven't totalled up the bill yet. Rusty was funny. He did make me laugh."

"Then next time try getting a joke book from the library. It would be cheaper. A lot cheaper."

Cyn sighed. "I suppose. Although I should have taken

your advice and pushed for a prenuptial agreement. Maybe the divorce wouldn't have cost quite so much. It just seemed so terribly unromantic. And Rusty was dead set against it."

"I'm not surprised. I don't suppose he had anything much to lose, now did he?"

"Anyway, I was calling to find out if you were coming back up to New York for my father's birthday. He's in Europe on business, but he'll be back for his surprise party. He promised."

Jo chewed on her lip. Jeremiah Fox was Cyn's father; he had more or less unofficially adopted Jo when her own father had passed away. After an unfortunate second marriage, her mother, Anne Gordon Sharpe, had called it quits on the married life and resolved to stay single.

Cyn, meanwhile, had abandoned her father's name of Fox and taken on Savene after her first husband. At the time of their divorce, Cyn had confided that the name was the only thing she had liked in the whole arrangement and had clung to it ever since.

Cyn cleared her throat, bringing Jo back to the present.

"I'm not sure, Cyn. Let me check. I'm kind of involved in a couple of things at the store right now. It's our busy season. And I've just adopted a homeless cat. Literally."

"Think about it. You could see Glen again, too. I'm sure my father wouldn't mind if I invited him. Gigantic, charismatic publisher with lots of money . . ."

"I would mind!" Jo snapped angrily. "Our divorce is almost final. All that he has to do is sign the papers."

"Maybe he doesn't want to be divorced. When I saw him he certainly didn't look particularly happy. He was all alone!"

"Poor Mr. Howard. He's just going to have to get used to it." Jo paused. "Look, Cyn. I'll get back to you about that party. I may be going south to scuba during the week. I'll call when I return."

"Uh, glub, glub. You're welcome to it. I hate the water. And I hate being under the water. I can honestly say the only water I do like is when I'm looking at it from aboard a cruise ship. A very expensive cruise ship!"

"Didn't your Number Two take you on a cruise for your honeymoon? Arnold or Art or . . ."

"Archie, dear. Like in the comic strip. It was how he made his living. Drawing comic strips that never sold." Cyn emitted a long sigh. "At least we had a nice honeymoon, courtesy of my father, of course."

"Naturally. I have an idea! Why don't you come down for a week or two? There are other things to do besides swim and dive. Remember the fun we had together that time I was in New York? We went to Radio City and led a charge on the men's bathroom when the women's was so crowded during intermission? You stood guard at the door while I directed traffic inside. Some poor guy hopped up and down on one foot because you wouldn't let him in?"

Cyn's throaty laugh sounded over the line. "Oh, for the good old days!" Then she sighed. "I honestly wish I could say yes, but . . . I think that peace and quiet would likely kill me. Vegetating isn't my line. Oh, my other phone's ringing. Think about that party. O.K.?"

"All right. But no promises. I really . . ."

But Cyn was gone, already moving on to someone else.

". . . don't want to run into my ex. Or soon-to-be ex," Jo finished softly.

Jo wondered if she would ever get to the point where hearing Glen's name wouldn't cause some kind of intense reaction inside of her. She hoped so. And very soon. She needed to put Glen Howard and her life in New York behind her. Once and for all.

Jo snatched up her purse after locking the diary into a desk drawer. The telephone began shrilling in her cubicle of an office. She galloped toward the door as Tara answered.

"It's your husband!" Tara mouthed as Jo dived past. "What do you want me to say?"

"I'm out," the other woman muttered, bolting through the door like a rabbit down its hole. As Jo let the screen snap back with a loud bang, she added her final word: "Permanently!"

Chapter Four

'The time has come,' the Walrus said,
'To talk of many things' . . .
—Lewis Carroll, *Through the Looking-
Glass and What Alice Found there*

Jo drove her small-sized Chevy slowly back up Oregon
Inlet Road and north on Virginia Dare Trail. It was a beautiful May day for a drive up to Corolla and the Currituck
Lighthouse on the Outer Banks. She followed Route 158
past the wind-swept dunes of Jockey Ridge State Park and
the white, stark memorial to the Wright Brothers and their
first flight at Kitty Hawk, then followed the road which ran
like an arthritic finger through the peninsula.

Before she knew it, Jo could see the Currituck Lighthouse climbing upward into the cloud-strewn sky. The research facility was directly across from the yellow mansion
that had been known as the Whalehead Club, one of the
hunt clubs located on Currituck Sound. Jo followed a
wooded road down toward the water. A white clapboard
sign directed her to the parking lot for the aquarium and
research building.

Jo paused and stopped to study the building. It was huge
with multiple glassed-in gables on the roof. The yellow and
white-trimmed structure hung out over a portion of the

sound. As Jo exited her car and walked closer, she could see what looked like a surfboat tied up at a rear dock.

The receptionist was tall, blonde, and obviously a college student, possibly with a major in Marine Biology. She had the fresh-scrubbed innocent look that Jo often associated with Tara Cataldo. Like Tara, she was friendly as an over-grown puppy.

"Mr. Switec? He'll be along shortly. He's conducting a fund-raiser in the Neptune Auditorium for one of the aquar-ium's new programs. We're a sponsor for the exploration of Blackbeard's *Queen Anne's Revenge* down in the Beau-fort Harbor area. But I know he'd like to talk to you." She ran her eyes assessingly over Jo's slender form. "He is our resident expert on the Blackbeard phenomenon down here on the Outer Banks. Even dresses up like him in the annual pageant over on Ocracoke in conjunction with the museum there."

"Why don't I just look around until he's finished then? If you'll tell him I'm here?"

The girl nodded cheerily and went back to typing and frowning at her computer screen. Jo wandered across a spa-cious lobby, complete with a purple and peach fountain, and into the corridor past the inevitable gift shop. Soothing sea sounds were being piped through the facility from a tape on the loud speaker system. Beyond the gift shop, Jo spotted two classrooms with small-sized desks, intended for schoolchildren.

The first large aquarium tank had a sign "Fish Finder Guide to North Carolina." Jo noted the dark shadows of black sea bass, the sharp-nosed snout of the barracuda, and the florescent color of an amberjack, while in the next room a large tank of alligators lazily sprawled around several small pools of water. A catwalk ran along the top of the exhibit, which was likely used for feeding.

The "Close Encounters" fishtank in the farthest room was the most exciting. The gray-brown bodies and deadly sharp teeth of the shark exhibit made Jo think of the great white shark in *Jaws*. The sharks glided effortlessly in their oversized pool. There was another catwalk above the tank with a red warning sign, "Repairs in Progress—Keep Off."

Two of the sharks bumped into the glass, close to where Jo was standing. She jumped back and stared as the closest tiger shark flashed a full set of pearly teeth at her.

"My, what big teeth you have, Grandma," Jo mumbled to herself.

"All the better to eat you with, my dear."

Someone was standing directly behind her. Jo swung around to confront a darkly handsome, smiling man, who according to his name badge was the absent Mr. Switec. He was wearing a casual plaid shirt and slacks, but his eyes were what fascinated Jo. They were black and seemed to bore a hole straight through her; eyes so dark it seemed that they were all pupil.

"So what do you think of our tiger sharks, Ms . . ."

"Sharpe. Jo Sharpe. And I think . . ." her gaze returned to the glass, "they have an abundance of teeth!"

He laughed, not a titter, but a hearty sound. "They do have twenty rows of serrated teeth. Although you need not worry about finding one around here. They are located generally in the tropics."

"I'm glad. I'd hate to run into one of these fellows underwater!"

"Underwater? You dive, then?"

"Yes. I married a local fellow and learned. I find the sea fascinating."

A shadow crossed his dark-skinned face. "And your husband? He dives too?"

"No. He never liked it. But it's strange; he's good at it. He's good at everything. Except staying married."

"So . . . I was right. When I saw you standing, watching the fish, you seemed . . . unattached. Uninvolved. You're divorced, then?"

Jo frowned. "Soon-to-be. As soon as I can pin down my dearly ex-beloved and get his signature on the divorce papers." She paused. "But what about you? Successful author, scuba diver. Are you involved with the dive on the *Queen Anne's Revenge* too?"

"Yes. I've been invited along. I run the library on the dive boat. Plus cataloguing and keeping track of everything the divers recover from the ocean floor. Are you interested in Blackbeard?"

"Oh, more than you'll ever know." Jo saw him glance at his watch. "I'm sorry, Mr. Switec. It's nice of you to see me on such short notice. I haven't told you the reason for my interest in Blackbeard. And the *Queen Anne's Revenge*."

In a few terse sentences, she told him about her finding the diary and the history of Cristabel Lamonte.

Norm smiled. "I see. It seems your interest in Blackbeard is considerably more than the casual tourist. Perhaps we could get some lunch at the Whalehead Club. And maybe add a climb of the lighthouse steps into the bargain. There's a fantastic view of the Currituck Sound."

Jo grinned. "I'd like that. You really don't mind answering a lot of questions about Blackbeard?"

"Not at all. But only if you call me Norm. I keep looking around for my father every time I hear 'Mr. Switec.' "

"Deal." Jo held out her hand to formally shake on it.

Norm had been right, Jo thought happily to herself. The view from the Currituck Lighthouse was fabulous. It had been a long climb of over two hundred stairs on a dizzy spiral staircase inside the lighthouse, but it was worth it. Jo looked out at the silky smooth water as the sun danced across the sound, the rays like myriad fairies at play. The birds were dark silhouettes over the distant town of Currituck on the far shore; the winged creatures reminded Jo more of bats than the gulls and egrets they actually were.

Now Jo stared across the table at Norm over their lunch at the Whalehead Club. He had not followed her up the spiral staircase of the lighthouse, claiming a fear of heights as the cause.

Norm's eyes followed a flock of geese as they nested under the oak trees which bordered the nearby road.

"Look at them, Jo. Those geese. Aren't they beautiful? Although it's nothing like when migration time comes in

December and January. Then there are thousands of swans, ducks, snow geese, cormorants and widgeons. These few are just some happy campers who decided to hang around for the summer rather than flying north."

"You sound like you are very attached to the animals." Jo slurped at her crab soup, her eyes on Norm's face.

"In certain ways they are nicer than people. Animals don't turn on one another and force them to become outcasts. They don't destroy each other for no better motive than jealousy, envy, or revenge."

She had the feeling Norm had changed gears, from talking about the animals to talking about people. Jo studied him as he turned to claim the check from the elderly volunteer who tried to slide it unobtrusively across the table.

Norm glanced at the amount, stuck a bill under the server, and shoved it away. Then he looked Jo straight in the eyes.

"We've talked about everything but Blackbeard. And. . . . a diary you said you've found?"

Jo nodded wordlessly.

"Blackbeard happens to be a rather flamboyant figure in pirate history. Possibly the most famous pirate of all time. And information about him and his den on Ocracoke is relatively well-known. Not like his pirate buddy, Stede Bonnet. Now that fellow will remain an enigma for all time."

"Pirate buddy? You mean a cutthroat like Blackbeard actually had friends?"

"In the beginning. But hang on and I'll start way back when and tell you the whole tale. Or as much of it as history knows."

Jo settled in her chair. Their waitress had left, along with the check. She took a sip of her iced tea.

"I'm all ears. So tell me about the most famous pirate that ever lived."

And he did.

Two hours later, Jo's head was spinning over facts from Blackbeard's life: friendships, loyalty of his crew, and betrayal by another pirate friend named Stede Bonnet.

"How can I ever thank you? It would have taken me hours to look all of this up." Jo smiled her gratitude.

Norm stared out over the white glassy water of Currituck Sound, but she had a feeling that the man wasn't even aware of the scenery.

He turned abruptly. "Actually, there is something I'd like. That diary. Do you suppose I could see it? There has to be a clue about the treasure somewhere. Perhaps the pirates were further south, toward Cedar Island. One of the legends about the place is that Blackbeard was finally buried there, although that doesn't agree with other accounts of his demise. And we need to be very sure that it was Blackbeard who did the kidnapping."

"Cristabel talked about seeing the pirate's flag—a black banner with a white skeleton and a heart filled with a drop of red blood. Does it sound familiar?"

Norman glanced at Jo sharply, as though making up his mind about something. "It sounds like Cristabel has gotten under your skin. Or into your blood, shall we say?"

Jo laughed. "Perhaps she did. It's the story of legends. Young, beautiful girl, black-hearted pirate. But there was no happy ending. Definitely not a Paul Henreid and Maureen O'Hara romance."

"No. Look, I'm going down to Beaufort later this afternoon. After the fund-raiser here. Do you think . . . I know it's short notice, but would you like to see the *Queen Anne's Revenge?* I have complete authorization to get you out on the dive boat. You can examine the relics. If you know how to dive . . ."

Jo nodded, her face beginning to glow with anticipation. "My bookstore assistant mentioned the site. Perhaps you know her. Tara Cataldo."

"Yes, I know Tara. One of our most dedicated workers. So you can explore the site. Also the library on the dive boat. It's rather extensive, if I do say so myself. As a matter of fact, the entire dive boat is rather extensive."

Jo hesitated. The idea of exploring an original pirate shipwreck underwater and helping to authenticate a find of this magnitude was very tempting. And Norm had gone out of his way to be helpful, making himself available from a busy schedule and treating her to lunch.

"Do say yes. Your assistant can take care of your cat. At least for one night. I'll have a chance to examine that diary! And you will have an opportunity of a lifetime to explore an original pirate vessel underwater."

"Opportunity knocks." Jo laughed suddenly. "You're right. I'd love to dive the *Queen Anne's Revenge*. If I leave early tomorrow, I'll be down to Beaufort by mid-day."

"Until then," Norman Switec said softly. "I'm counting on you, Jo. Blackbeard's ship and cannon and pieces of eight . . ."

"Pieces of eight, huh? How could I possibly resist?" Jo answered her own question. "I can't. Until tomorrow. And don't you dare find all of the pieces of eight before I get there!"

Chapter Five

I viewed the ocean green,
—Coleridge, *Rime of the Ancient Mariner*

Josephine Sharpe left early for Beaufort the following morning with the light just peeking up over the deep bluish gray waters of the Albemarle Sound. The clouds had been a soft cobweb-gray, illuminated by the sun first appearing on the horizon as Jo drove rapidly overland and southward, past the turnoff to the picturesque fishing village of Wanchese, through New Bern and on to the Victorian city of Beaufort. Norm had met her in front of the Maritime Museum and had ferried Jo, plus her overnight bag, out to the luxurious cruise ship that was serving as the headquarters for the divers on the *Queen Anne's Revenge*.

After giving Jo the grand tour of the dive ship with its ultra-deluxe dining room, French chef, gorgeous staterooms, research library, and a doctor plus hospital, Norm had escorted her to a beautiful cabin. He confided that service would be especially good since a V.I.P. sponsor of Scisearch, who probably didn't know the bow from the stern, had just checked into a suite on the upper deck. Looking around at the first class refitting of the ship, Jo couldn't have cared less.

Now she cleared her diving mask of bubbles and eased the regulator into her mouth. Norman Switec had been as

44

good as his word about letting her dive the *Queen Anne's Revenge,* although he seemed to be most unhappy about her not bringing Cristabel's diary on board. Then Jo shrugged and put it out of her mind. She had a number of other things to worry about at the moment.

Jo slipped down into the water with the weight-belt hugging her waist and a black scuba tank filled with air attached behind her buoyancy compensator vest. Off to her left, her partner followed closely on her trail.

Jo hadn't really had a chance to say more than a casual hello to Quintin Addison, her shadowed diving companion. Norm had bowed out of diving, claiming an ear infection, but Quint seemed a good substitute. He was a typically clean-cut, blond, all-collegiate type, who was majoring in marine biology at North Carolina State and was spending his summer doing what he liked best, which was diving. He assisted Jo with her equipment, insisted she use his Scubapro regulator, which she was more familiar with, and even offered an extra five pound weight on her belt to assist with buoyancy, saying that he had observed that very slender women had less trouble floating than men.

Jo wondered idly what Norman Switec had told him. Probably that she was a rank amateur that he should watch out for, regardless of the fact that Jo held her diver's certification and they were only going to be down to a twenty-foot depth. Most diving accidents occurred at much deeper depths, due to decompression problems or equipment failure. In spite of it all, Jo was going to dive Blackbeard's flagship and that was most important.

Jo sank below the surface, a trail of bubbles following her down. She took a long pull on the air in her regulator and began breathing normally. The sunlight disappeared as the reds and oranges at the surface faded to light blue and then violet. In mere seconds, Jo was down on the silty, sandy bottom, Quint close behind her.

She peered around. Visibility was quite good, considering the fact that the wreck was on one of the shoales. Directly off to one side and barely in her line of vision was a black-clad diver using a hand-fanning device, a dredge, and an airlift. Jo watched the sand as it blew back, disclosing part of what could have been one of the forty cannons Blackbeard had mounted when he refitted the *Queen Anne's Revenge*.

She ventured closer, then felt a tap on her shoulder. Quint was shaking his head in a negative sign, so Jo turned away to explore the rest of the site.

The artifacts were spread out in a half-circular pattern. Part of what looked like the stern of the ship sat toward the starboard side, while what looked like part of the bow was partially erect. A long stretch of the wooden hull was also visible on the far side. A school of translucent, blue pompano swam close to the cannons, which were sprawled in the sand like gigantic pick-up-sticks every which way. Above her head, Jo caught the long ripple movement of a barracuda with its gleaming teeth, trailing the pompano. Even the amberjacks and groupers gave the barracuda with his lethal, knife-like incisors, a wide birth.

Jo swam forward, past the diver and his airlift. A section of the rotted hull lay before her, holes punched in the side, looking like a piece of brown Swiss cheese. Beyond the hull was a section of what must have been the anchor, sticking partially out of the silty bottom.

Jo crossed over to the opposite side of the wreck, pulling air off the regulator. Her legs were beginning to ache from the strain of propelling herself through the water with the black fins on her feet. She saw a crab mincing along the bottom, along with a slithering red, brown, and white lizard-type of fish that reminded her of a water version of an iguana she had once seen at the zoo. Black piles of ballast stones were spread across the right side of the sand surrounding the wreck. Jo stopped for a closer look and spotted a fan-shaped body with two eyes peering up at her. It was a Southern stingray, partially concealed on the bottom with only the bulbous eyes protruding up out of the skin. Jo carefully gave the dark, spotted body a wide berth before checking her dive watch, another loan from Quint.

They had been under for almost thirty minutes. Jo hastened toward the last cannon, located far to the left of the other fifteen or so that had been discovered. She knew that she would have to hurry; her breath was coming in shorter gasps and suddenly she felt incredibly tired. Jo reached the last cannon and looked down. The date, 1709, was just visible underneath the barnacles encrusting the gun. She reached and had almost touched the cannon when she saw it.

A gigantic manta ray swam past, its ugly, deformed body almost brushing her arm. Jo pulled back sharply, as the regulator was yanked from her mouth, hit the cannon, and floated free.

Her eyes widened behind the black scuba mask as she exhaled air in a panic and stared at the ray. Probing, devil-eyes glimmered back before he turned and skittered along the bottom, away from her and the cannon. Jo grabbed for the regulator as water began to fill her nose and mouth. She jammed the plastic behind her teeth and cleared the mask. But the air didn't flow smoothly. Jo heard herself gasping as she fought for breath. The regulator must have been damaged. The seconds ticked past. She had a feeling of light-headedness as a black, spotted curtain descended over her eyes. Vaguely she felt hands grasping at her as a different regulator was forced into her mouth. As the air reached her lungs, Jo began to breath normally and her vision cleared.

Quint was by her side along with the black-clad diver minus his air gun, which had been dropped over by the cannon in the center of the wreck. Quint's regulator was the one she was breathing on. Jo filled her lungs and passed it back to him. Together they kept "buddy-breathing" as Jo dropped her weight-belt into the sand and rose slowly toward the surface. Quint passed her the regulator again and she drew another long breath. The dark pinwheels of black vanished from in front of her eyes. The younger diver supported both of them, as the colors of the water changed back to the red and yellow of the surface. Then there was a flurry of white and silver bubbles as Jo gasped air. Two heads broke the surface as the dazzling warm sun flooded the sea with welcome light.

Jo looked around, bleary-eyed. She could see a skiff being launched from the nearby dive boat. But how had Norman Switec known of her mishap? Of course, the video cameras had been following her every step of the way. The skiff shot over the waves, white foam churning up a wake. Norm reached down as Quint boosted Jo into the smaller boat.

She sprawled in the bottom, feeling like a fish suddenly out of water. Jo eased the scuba tank off her back, as Quint clambered onboard. Norm turned the skiff back toward the dive boat.

"What happened?"

Jo realized the question was directed toward Quint.

"A manta ray under one of the cannons. Her regulator jammed, that's all. It's no big deal."

Jo raised her head and studied the two men. Norm looked angry, Quint defensive. She laid a hand, tentatively, on Norm's shoulder as the skiff reached the dive boat.

"He's right, Norm. It could happen to anyone. That's why it's a good idea to have a diving partner. You know that yourself."

"Yes, but . . ." Norm stopped. "You'd best relax and stay over at least until tomorrow. No point driving back when you're not well."

"I was going to do that anyway. I just need to lay down for a bit and I'll be fine." Jo smiled at Quint encouragingly. "Nothing really happened thanks to Quint here."

The younger man seemed mollified. Norm bit his lip and looked as though he wanted to say a great deal more, but didn't. He tied the skiff up to the dive boat and Quint helped Jo aboard.

"Thanks," the younger diver murmured in her ear. "Tara said you were okay for a person over thirty. I think she was right!"

"You know Tara well?"

Quint nodded. "She called earlier. Actually, she kind of asked me to watch out for you, since you were a special friend." He assisted Jo over the gunwale of the dive boat. "I'm just glad I was there."

"I'm glad too, Quint. Listen, I'll see you both at dinner in the main banquet salon. I'm going to rest for now."

Jo left the scuba mask, fins, and compensator lying on the deck as she trailed back through the library in her bare feet and wet bathing suit to her cabin.

Jo opened the unlocked door, eased inside, and slipped out of the bathing suit and into the shower. Then her body started shaking violently, uncontrollably, with the reaction from her dive. She turned the hot water on and stood still, as the pellets of spray flowed over her.

The shaking finally stopped as Jo turned off the water, donned the fancy bathrobe hanging on the back of the door, and collapsed onto the bed. Exhaustion flowed over her like the waves from the translucent sea and she slept.

Chapter Six

The sweeping up the Heart,
And putting love away
We shall not want to use again
Until Eternity.
                    —Emily Dickinson

J o dreamed she was back in New York in the penthouse
she and Glen had shared overlooking Central Park. But
Glen was off in London at Ho-Jo's British central office
and Jo was alone, wandering through the empty rooms. The
maid and cook had both left early, to celebrate the holidays
with their family. Even Roland, the driver that Glen had
insisted upon, was gone, along with her bodyguard. Jo finally collapsed by the lopsided Christmas tree and stared
at the television set, showing a massive crowd of happy,
cheery people in Times Square. *Perhaps if I open the front
door,* Jo thought, *and break open Glen's liquor cabinet,
someone will come inside and keep me company.* There
hadn't even been a telephone call from Glen, since a storm
in London had caused power outages throughout the city.
No planes were taking off and her husband would be stuck
there for at least a couple of days.

The doorbell chime from the security desk on the first
floor rang sharply. Jo had dragged herself upright and
peered into the video camera to see a grinning Cyn waving

a bottle of Bollanger along with two glasses. Jo sprang into life and rang her up.

"I hope I'm not interrupting." Cyn's sharp-eyed gaze searched the apartment and came up empty of people, except for Jo. "But when you said you were alone . . ."

"Sit down! Glen's stuck in London again. We can talk about old times. Let's go in by the tree and you can tell me what's happening."

Cyn shrugged out of her chinchilla coat and flung it over a leather-backed armchair. She put the two glasses on the black marble coffee table, popped the cork on the Bollanger, and filled the glasses with bubbly.

The two friends stared out of the gigantic picture window with its view of the light-speckled city stretched below. Cyn eased back into the comfy armchair and glanced around.

"I always did like this room," she murmured, sliding her alligator shoes off her feet and stretching her legs out.

Jo looked up from the stereo-VCR combination, where Christmas music was playing softly. "I've always thought it was rather cold myself."

Cyn studied the priceless Degás over the fireplace, which Glen had purchased the previous year in Paris. "I'll take this kind of cold any day, any time," she muttered, "along with that picture if you ever get tired of looking at it."

Jo studied the picture dispassionately. "You could have it now if it were up to me. Ballerinas in tutus, drifting around hither and yon like pink snowflakes on parade have never been my cup of tea. But . . ." she finished hastily, "Glen said he likes the thing. And unless you have the money, the insurance on it would kill you."

Cyn had been looking hopeful, but she dropped her head and studied the bubbles in her glass. "That's one thing you don't have to worry about: money. It's been a major issue between Harry and me since day one. He actually had the nerve to tell me I spend too much on clothes. One has to dress, for Pete's sake."

Jo thought about Harry, Cyn's third husband. Half-bald with a hairline that had been retreating for years. But

Cyn had taken one look and decided Harry was for her. Or perhaps it was his bank book which had been for her. Regardless, Harry had turned into a good-for-nothing tightwad as far as Cyn was concerned. Jo half-listened as her friend rambled on about Harry closing her charge accounts after she had purchased a little million dollar beach shack on Long Island for their summer vacations.

Cyn stopped rambling and studied Jo. "You don't look terribly happy. As a matter of fact, you look like you're the one with two failed marriages. And you're not drinking the Bollanger. Don't you like it?"

"No. It's fine. But the doctor told me I'm not supposed to drink in . . . er . . . my condition."

"Condition?" Cyn's pupils narrowed to black slits in her jungle green eyes. "You mean you're expecting a little one?" She took a long swallow of champagne. "Does the absent Mr. Howard know yet?"

"Uh-uh." Jo pulled her long legs under her as she shook her head. "I was going to tell him when he got home from London. I just found out myself. It wasn't something I wanted to do on the telephone. But now . . ." She turned to the arched picture window as white snowflakes pinwheeled down.

"Don't worry, Jo." Cyn gulped down her own drink and started on her friend's. "I'll be here for you. Trust me. We've always stood together through thick and thin. Remember when we first met, after my family moved in next door? You came home from college and found that nasty little snot from across the way teasing me with a garter snake? Miss Mustache he called me, because of my hairlip. Do you recollect what you did?"

Jo wracked her brain, but the incident had made more of an impression on Cyn than on her.

"Er . . . not exactly."

"You shoved him over into your mother's flower bed and jammed the snake down his shirt front. Your mother saw him jumping around all over her petunias, called his parents, and had him grounded for six months! You were there for me then and I'm here for you now. Just because you've got a negligent husband . . ."

Jo roused herself, feeling it her duty to defend Glen. "Not really, Cyn. He's just never home when I need somebody. Here I am, stuck alone in this God-awful big apartment, alone on New Year's Eve."

Cyn cradled her friend's hand in her own.

Jo stirred in sleep. She could almost feel her friend holding her hand tightly, as though she would never let it go. Yet the voices Jo heard in the background weren't female but male, and they were arguing violently.

"I don't understand how you could have let this happen, Switec," the deep resonant voice snarled out. "I told you to watch out and be careful in that damned wreck. You know how precious Jo is to me! She was almost killed!"

Norman Switec's voice cut in, whining and defensive. "But it's not a serious accident. It wasn't like she was down a hundred feet in a cave using trimex gas. A fish startled her and knocked the regulator out of her mouth, for God's sake. She and Quint were only down twenty-two feet when it happened!"

Norman Switec continued. "Besides, I didn't know she was your wife. How could I? She said her last name was Sharpe. There's no wedding ring and she said she was getting a divorce!"

"I just don't understand why two grown men would have such trouble keeping tabs on one lone woman." Suddenly the second voice sounded infinitely weary, almost desolate. "It's so dangerous down there!"

Jo stirred. She recollected Norm's words about having "a VIP sponsor of Scisearch, who just checked into the deluxe suite on the upper deck" aboard. There was a strong, sinking feeling in the pit of Jo's stomach. She suddenly, positively knew who the VIP in the deluxe suite had to be; the person who "didn't know the bow from the stern on a boat."

She opened her eyes and stared at the long brown tapered fingers holding her hand.

"Hello, Glen. Imagine running into you here of all places."

He seemed exactly as she remembered: the strong chin, dark locks of hair hanging over his forehead, and the liquid brown eyes. Although maybe not. Now the eyes seemed tired, and in them there was an expression not just of concern, but something else. Despair, perhaps?

"You see, Mr. Howard. She's fine!" Norman Switec wiped his forehead with a rumpled, used piece of tissue. His black, protruding eyes inspected Jo.

"Tell him, Jo. Tell Mr. Howard you're okay!"

Jo centered back on her soon-to-be ex-husband. "I'm okay, *Mr. Howard,*" she said parroting what Norman Switec had said.

Quint hovered doubtfully in the background, as though now unsure whether to stay or leave.

"I should have known it was you." Jo's brow furrowed in thought. "Who else would re-do an entire cruise ship to be used as a dive boat?"

"Well, it was only a small cruise ship. It sailed the Alaskan coast. Great for getting into small, tight harbors." Glen dismissed the other men with a wave of his arm. Quint and Norman Switec almost ran into each other in their haste to get through the cabin door at the same time.

Glen watched their departure. "Your two rescuers seem to have abandoned ship."

"Pity you don't join them." Jo eased herself slowly upright on the bed. Her leg muscles contracted painfully from the strain of her earlier underwater adventure.

"What are you doing here anyway? I didn't think you liked water."

"I don't, except to bathe in," Glen responded smoothly. "I decided to come down and see about my investment. Scisearch has spent a small bundle in financing the salvage of the wreck."

"And I bet you wanted to be certain you were getting your money's worth!"

"I should think you would be glad. You and Cyn both seem to have no trouble spending money. Just making it."

"It won't be your concern once those divorce papers are signed. Oh!" Jo exclaimed in fury. "I don't have them along. I wasn't expecting . . ."

"You weren't expecting what, Josephine? My charming presence down here?"

It came to her rather irrelevantly that Glen was the only person who ever used her full first name.

"I know how you detested it here. Remember when we visited Ocracoke after our wedding?"

Glen shifted uneasily. "Perhaps I was a bit harsh. But I'd worked like a dog to make something of myself. And I just couldn't feel comfortable going back. Call it insecurity. Call it whatever you want. But the feeling was there."

Jo swung herself off of the high Victorian four-poster bed. Her feet dug into the dark red, plush carpeting. She gathered up her shoes and staggered toward the bathroom.

"Are you sure you should be up and about already? There's still some time before dinner in the main salon. You could rest."

"I'm not staying for dinner. I'm getting off this floating pleasure palace right now!"

"Now Josephine? You can't." Glen leaned back on the high-backed chair next to the fireplace. His slitted eyes watched Jo thoughtfully in the mirror.

"What do you mean, I can't?" Jo's voice was dangerously quiet.

"It's like this, the skiff that brought you out to the dive boat has gone back to shore. It won't be out again until tomorrow."

"You kidnapped my skiff and sent it ashore?"

"It's not your skiff, dear, it's mine. And yes, I sent it ashore. It seemed like a good idea at the time."

"In other words, I'm marooned here!"

Glen laughed. "Don't get all dramatic on me! You're not stranded on a desert island, but on a luxurious cruise ship! I've even provided some guests for entertainment over dinner."

"Guests?" Jo slammed the dresser drawer. "You planned

this whole thing. You manipulated all of us. How did you know I would be here? I wasn't sure I was coming myself. And neither was Norm."

"Now, Josephine, you don't expect me to give away all my secrets, do you?"

"I suppose it was Cyn. She's busy planning marriage number five with whats-his-name and wants everyone else to be happy too."

"I have an update. When I talked to Cyn, husband-to-be number five—I think his name is Eric—seemed to have bolted and headed for the far hills. Very far."

Jo's mouth twisted in a bitter line. "Neither one of us seems to have had much luck in the way of husbands."

"There's still hope. Don't count yourself out yet." Glen slid off the corner of the bed. "Or Cyn either." He paused. "I've arranged dinner for eight o'clock. Is that all right? I know you like to eat later. And your wish is my command."

"Does it really matter what I like, Glen? Especially in regard to time. You seemed to have little enough of it for me before."

"Of course it does, Josephine. Sometimes I'm just not so great at expressing it." He paused, then added lightly, "Besides, lack of time is one of the downsides of marrying a successful man. If you'd have married some poor slob without a nickle to his name, he would have been hanging around your neck like the ill-fated albatross. Why, you could have even happily supported him. Many women do these days. Mister X and Josephine living in their garret!"

Jo misunderstood. "Everything comes back to money with you, now doesn't it? It's all you're interested in."

"But oh, how you do enjoy spending it." Glen eased himself over to the door. "You and that barracuda friend of yours. She goes through wealthy men as fast as most people go through dinner!"

Jo's mouth twisted in a bitter grimace and the memories flooding through her mind made her cruel. "Leave Cyn out of this. It's a shame that you weren't half as interested in staying around as she was. Maybe," and here Jo drew a deep breath, "our daughter would be alive today if you'd made yourself a little more available."

Glen's face whitened under his tan. "I'll say one thing for the North Carolina sea and sun, your spiteful tongue seems to have flourished. Tell me Josephine, has it developed since you came down here or were you always so naturally vicious?"

"Get out!"

"With pleasure." His footsteps sounded loud on the parquet floor of the cabin. And then the door opened and shut, leaving Jo alone in the room, with only the haunting memories of a dark-haired little girl, and what might have been, to keep her company.

Chapter Seven

The guests are met, the feast is set;
May'st hear the merry din.
—Samuel Taylor Coleridge, *Rime
of the Ancient Mariner*

Jo was one of the last ones down to dinner in the elegant
Romanov dining salon. A long central table, simply laid,
graced the center of the room, flanked by two waiters to
fetch and carry delicacies from the kitchen. The room was
decorated with ornate red and gold wallpaper, a faux blue
ceiling, golden columns, and a central fireplace. Jo joined
the other guests and the crew mingling around the bar at
the far end of the table.

She had changed into a simple black dress and Stuart
Weitzman heels that Cyn had helped her select from Vera
Wang in New York. Jo had added a double strand of choke
pearls a la Jackie Kennedy. Norman Switec gave an appre-
ciative look as he broke away from the rest of the group
with a glass of champagne in his hand.

"I hope bubbly is your drink. There is a full bar, if not.
I wasn't sure and your husband wasn't around to ask."

"My soon-to-be ex-husband." Jo's eyes scanned the
group for Glen's dark hair, tinged with gray at the temples.
"I don't see him around, Norm. Don't tell me we're not to
have the pleasure of his company at dinner?"

"No such luck. He went to help the snail expert get settled on board. I trust they will both be along shortly."

"Did you say snail expert?" Jo thought she had misunderstood. "Like the kind of snails you eat?"

Norm took a sip of his scotch. "Right. His name is Watson Wise." Norm made a grimace. "He even sounds like a snail expert. I saw him come on board. Small, dark, kind of like a little round pumpkin, but he's a writer and has published in the *Journal of Sea Research.* You'll have a chance to plumb the depths of his knowledge. Our expert is next to you at dinner."

Jo turned to look at the long table. Two chandeliers blazed brightly over the glittering glassware and china. Her eyes searched the dining room once more.

"So what do you think of our little floating palace?"

"Oh, the research library and facilities and your computer setup are fabulous. But this room is kind of . . ."

"Garish?" Norm supplied when Jo stopped. He studied the heavy red brocade draperies and the double-eagle design of the Romanov family of Russia on the back of each chair.

"Actually, your ex got the ship from a company that used to do a run up the Inside Passage of Alaska. Alaska was originally owned by the Russians during the Romanov Dynasty before they sold it to the United States. Hence the red, gold, and black motif." Norm leaned on one leg and winced. Jo glanced up in alarm.

"Are you okay? You look a little pale."

"Not to worry. I have cramping and ulcerating leg trouble. I can't get around as freely as I would like, is all."

"Should you be resting or something useful like that?"

"I wouldn't miss this gathering even if you offered to play Florence Nightingale," Norm responded stoutly. "But let's ease over to the dining table. I can tell you about the dinner guests. We have a very unique gathering here."

Norm pulled out one of the high-backed chairs for Jo before seating himself. A waiter discreetly filled up their water glasses.

"Aside from myself, we have Dr. Smita Baid, our resident expert in marine archeology. She's very attractive and was on television the other night. She's also a good friend of mine and of our snail expert, Watson Wise."

Jo nodded as Norm continued.

"Then there would be Quintin and Rocky Coke, who are both divers. You saw Rocky earlier. He was manning the air hose and skimming sand off the artifacts on the *Queen Anne's Revenge.*

"The captain, whose name is Edward Hornos, is semi-retired. This is supposed to be his last sea outing. Of course, he's been saying that for as long as I can remember. We also have a navigator, Phil Collins, and two more divers."

"You certainly seem to have a complete bio on your shipmates."

"Norm grinned. "I'm the research librarian so it goes with the territory, I suppose, to find out essential information about everyone. You never know when some small fact can turn out to be very useful."

Norm took a sip of scotch. "And now we come to our latest additions to the ship. Watson Wise, the snail expert. Also, a Janna Lawrence, who is a publicist for Scisearch, and editor of *Alive!* magazine, and a BeBe Blue, her assistant."

Jo nodded. "They both work for Ho-Jo Publications. I knew them in New York." BeBe Blue was an older, no-nonsense editor, who was notorious for running her office like some kind of military camp. She got the job done on time, no matter what. Jo could honestly never recall seeing the woman smile. It was a good thing Glen was not paying her to be pleasant; he was paying her to do a good job.

And Janna Lawrence! A golden blond with a figure like a fashion model! Jo fingered the strands of pearls at her neck. She was glad she had thrown the little black dress by Vera Wang into her overnight case.

Norm looked up suddenly. "Why, here comes our chief now." He pulled himself erect as Glen Howard and Janna Lawrence approached the table, followed by the others, rather like lemmings going home to roost. Jo told herself not to be unkind. Especially to the poor lemmings; they didn't deserve it.

"Josephine, Norman. I'm not sure if you've both met Janna, my chief publicist. She was kind enough to fly down and oversea some local photographs in the paper on the *Queen Anne's Revenge.*" Glen's voice was smooth and ever so urbane. It was hard to believe that he had been trading insults with her only an hour before.

"Josie! It's nice to see you again! And Mr. Switec! I've been hearing so much about you!" Janna flashed dark eyes lined with mascara at Norm, while Jo ground her teeth at the damage done to her name, which she loathed, since it reminded her of a camel.

Glen pulled out a chair and Janna settled, her flame-red dress cascading around her like petals on a flower. Jo saw a small, dark-eyed man seat himself on the other side of Janna, across from Norm. The snail expert, obviously. The attractive Dr. Smita Baid was seated on Jo's left.

Her soon-to-be ex-husband was at the far end of the table, with the captain, Edward Hornos, and the divers.

Dr. Baid addressed Jo across the appetizer of steamed crab. "Mr. Switec tells me that you are the successful owner of a bookstore and antiquities shop out on Nag's Head. I've always found the study of the local history in this area to be fascinating." She nibbled delicately at her crab. "I've often thought if I hadn't been a marine archeologist, I would have been a teacher of history."

Jo hesitated, but then plunged ahead. After all, the doctor might be able to help her understand what Cristabel Lamonte had been talking about in her diary.

"If that's the case, then maybe you could give me some additional insight on a diary that is in my possession."

"Diary?" Watson Wise, the fish expert, took a long gulp from the glass of vodka he had brought to the table. "Of what sort?"

"A young daughter of a plantation owner from Beaufort. She was kidnapped by Blackbeard the pirate, but escaped from his ship." Jo was vaguely conscious that Glen had stopped talking to Janna Lawrence and was watching her intently.

"That's hardly amazing. At least for that marauding Blackbeard. The fellow had twelve or fourteen wives, including one back in England. They should have called him Bluebeard, the way he treated women." Watson Wise gave a sharp bray of laughter at the end of this speech.

Norman Switec frowned and gave Wise a dark look. "Blackbeard was really a rather enlightened pirate for his time. His men sailed under a rather democratic articles of confederation, you know."

"Yes, and he blackmailed his best friend Stede Bonnet, and stole his flagship." Watson Wise took another long swallow of liquor. His face was beginning to flush and even his partially bald head seemed to perspire.

Jo could sense Glen frowning at the far end of the table, but Norman Switec was the person who spoke.

"Regardless, Blackbeard was betrayed himself. By Stede Bonnet. Although they both had a nasty end, one by hanging, the other in a battle at sea."

"Sorry. I forgot that the pirate's name is sacrosanct in this neck of the woods. Anywhere else, he would be considered a highway robber and nothing more. Er . . . excuse me," Watson Wise hiccuped loudly, "a seagoing pirate and piece of scum."

Jo slid into the breach. "But that isn't what makes the diary so interesting. Cristabel talks about seeing the pirates hiding their treasure. Chests. She describes the site."

There was a stillness at their end of the table. Then Janna Lawrence spoke up.

"But did she give a location, Josie? You know, a map or something?"

"No. Just that the treasure was buried under some sort of 'poison tree.' "

"Poison, as in ivy?" Dr. Baid queried.

"The same." Jo turned to the marine archeologist. "Do you have any idea what she was referring to?"

The Indian woman frowned. Her golden yellow and brown sari shimmered in the chandeliers' light as she shook her head slowly. "I have never heard of such a thing. What about you, Watson?"

Wise steepled his hands on the table. "Community dynamics of sea creatures is really my forte. Particularly snails and predators like crayfish. I've never heard of something like a poison tree. But as I said, snails are more up my alley."

Glen Howard leaned back thoughtfully in his chair. "It might be worthwhile to finance a sort of treasure hunt if a location could be pinned down."

"And we could take pictures of the sites where the digging occurs," Janna piped up.

Jo looked at the other woman in disgust. Money and publicity. Did either of these two ever think of anything else? Did they even care about anything else? Jo doubted it.

The appetizer had long since disappeared, and was followed by the main course, a local white fish dipped in sauce. Jo picked at her food, thinking that some people, specifically her ex and Janna Lawrence, never changed.

Norman Switec gave her a sympathetic look. Out of all the people present, he seemed to understand how she felt. *Protective* was the word. She felt protective of a young girl's private thoughts and feelings. A young girl who had lived almost three hundred years ago, but who really wasn't so very different from women today.

Dessert was a crème caramel topped with cognac. Watson Wise had another refill on his glass of vodka and proceeded to discuss the mating habits of snails with Dr. Baid. Norman Switec was watching Glen and Janna Lawrence with their heads together at the end of the table. Jo nibbled slowly on her crème caramel and tried not to think about her ex-husband. She caught Norm's eye.

"Let's take our coffee into the main salon. We can talk more privately there."

Jo smiled and rose as Norm reached for her chair. She was conscious of Janna staring openly and Glen glaring darkly, but suddenly she didn't care. Giving Norm a nod, she followed him out of the garish black and red dining room. Quint and the other divers were close behind along with Dr. Baid. Watson Wise hauled himself erect, staggered, and then followed the general exodus. The entire group began milling around a samovar that one of the waiters set up in the lounge.

Jo settled herself into one of the high-backed chairs. She saw Glen and Janna exit the dining room and begin mingling with the group. The blond woman made a blooming hostess, stopping to smile and chatter with one person after another. Jo could see her cap of shimmering hair weaving to and fro.

Suddenly, she looked across the samovar and saw Watson Wise. But this was not the bald-headed snail expert from dinner. He had taken one of the waiter's red coats and donned a long, black beard and hairpiece. He had woven matches similar to the ones the real Blackbeard had used to intimidate prisoners in the fake beard. Two swords, which Watson had removed from over the fireplace completed the picture. Quint had joined him. Watson threw the younger man a sword and the two faked a duel with each other.

"Look at that drunken sot," Norman Switec said in disgust. "That little runt doesn't even resemble Blackbeard."

Janna Lawrence clapped her hands, egging the men on. Watson hacked away with his sword, rather like he was killing snakes. Quint, far more sober, dodged skillfully. Sweat poured off of the older man's face, as the heat from the matches wound in his beard turned his complexion a dull red.

Jo took a sip of her coffee, as the two men darted and sprang at each other. A chair keeled over with a loud crash. Then Watson snatched up a red tablecloth and waved it like a matador at Quint.

"Toro, toro," he bellowed. "Come to Blackbeard!"

Quint pawed the ground with his feet, rather like a bull getting ready to charge. Jo heard several people applaud and laugh shrilly in the background. The drinks from the bar flowed freely.

She turned away from the spectacle in disgust as Quint

bore down on Watson Wise, knocking over a couple of the high-backed chairs in the process.

Jo spoke to Norm. "I'll see you on deck. I need to powder my nose and I definitely need some air."

The research librarian seemed engrossed in watching the snail expert make a fool of himself. Jo shrugged and moved across the room to the outside corridor. She turned and ran straight into a tall, dark figure, who steadied her with his hands.

"So here you are," Glen Howard said softly. "I was beginning to think you were never going to leave and I did so want to talk to you."

Jo frowned. "Shouldn't you be attending to the party? And your guests? After all, they are helping to put Scisearch on the map with their work on the *Queen Anne's Revenge*."

"They seem to be having a good enough time on their own." His gaze traveled past Jo's head. "And where is the boyfriend? Is he playing chase the bull too?"

"You always did have a mouth on you. They are just having a little fun."

"That's generous of you. Especially considering that supposed accident when you were diving."

Jo straightened sharply. "What do you mean, 'supposed?' The regulator malfunctioned after it got knocked out of my mouth. It does happen."

"The thing seemed to be functioning perfectly when I saw it."

"Oh, are you an expert on diving now too?"

"No. I had Rocky Coke check it out once he surfaced with the air gun." He stared at her thoughtfully. "Be careful, Josephine. I don't like problems underwater."

"Are you saying it wasn't an accident? I don't believe it!"

"There's something strange about the whole thing. Can't you tell? It was just too convenient. Can't you feel the danger all around us?"

"I haven't felt any danger until now!" Jo pulled back,

away from Glen, her eyes large and brilliant in the half-light of the passageway.

Glen dropped his hands. "I'm sorry. I think I must have hurt you very badly at some point for you to be so suspicious of my motives now. Do you honestly think I could ever purposely hurt you?"

"You already have. You would just be putting the final touches on what happened after I lost the baby. But not to worry; people can't change their basic nature, I guess. And if it's in their basic nature to cause pain . . ."

His face contorted with agony, but then the door off the corridor opened.

"Are you here too, Jo? I was just on my way to the ladies' room." Dr. Smita Baid looked at Glen inquiringly. As Jo spun away, he turned back into the salon. The two women moved in the opposite direction.

"I hope I wasn't interrupting anything," Dr. Baid said carefully, her tone clipped and nonjudgmental.

"No, nothing of the slightest importance", Jo mumbled, following the older woman down the passageway to the door marked "The Empress Room." But she knew, even as she said it, that it wasn't true.

Dr. Baid paused. "If you are looking for a change in company, I saw that nice Mr. Switec going up on deck. I'm sure he would be delighted to see you."

Jo grinned. "How did you know I needed a change in the scenery?"

"Divorce is never easy. But sometimes it can be for the best." Smita Baid moved farther down the companionway. "Try the upper deck. The view of the shoreline is more romantic from there."

The door closed quietly behind her. Jo hesitated before turning to follow.

"Why not?" she muttered as she traced the companion-way, past the salon and up the stairs.

The air smelled of salt and the tang of the sea as the wind shifted off the northeast. The sea was an incarnadine color, and a white stab of lightning glittered like a silver sword far out on the water. It somehow reminded Jo of

Arthur's sword, Excalibur, disappearing into the realm of the Lady of the Lake in the ancient histories. Her eyes searched the deck. The vibrant colors of sunset had faded into a cobwebbed haze. Jo carefully moved toward the lone figure leaning on one leg by the railing.

"Look at it, Jo. Isn't this coastline one of the most beautiful you've ever seen?"

Jo turned obediently to peer out across the water. The miniature wavelets rose and fell like small lace handkerchiefs atop the black foam of the sea. The birds were quiet, having gone to nest until the next day.

Norm continued. "It's so peaceful here. Just the sea animals. There! See those dolphins? Their fins are outlined in the moonlight. They seem to be so happy, playing over the waves."

Jo leaned on the ship's railing. She studied Norm's profile in the half-light from the salon below them.

"I sometimes get the feeling that I would be happier dwelling with the fish at the aquarium than some of the people I have to butter up for money." He swung around to face Jo, his eyes almost protruding out of his head.

"I know. Rich people aren't particularly tactful. Especially when they are busy throwing their weight around."

"How true. But not just rich people. People in general. We are the only kind that will turn on those who are deformed or different. People are the only ones who will destroy their own."

"You don't like them much do you? These people living over there?" She indicated the far-off coastline.

"People are like lice, infecting the sea with pollution and the land with more pollution," Norm stated flatly, his tone brittle and dry. "Rachel Carson had the right idea. That's why they named the animal sanctuary on that island across from Beaufort after her."

"But people aren't all the same, you know. Some are good."

His mouth twisted bitterly. "The good ones get eaten alive or are so outnumbered they sink into oblivion, never to rise again."

"I'm sorry, Norm. It must be hard for you sometimes, collecting money for one thing or another." Jo edged closer to him. His dark, swarthy complexion reminded her once more of someone. Blackbeard, perhaps?

His head bent over hers. "I like you, Jo. You're so sane, so normal. Sometimes it seems like the whole world here has gone crazy. And yet . . ." He laughed suddenly. "I sound like Bogart in *Casablanca*. His line in the movie to Ingrid Bergman."

Jo thought back. "Something about the world not giving a damn about two little people?"

"That's us, Jo. The little people."

She looked into his eyes, those black, soft eyes. It seemed as though she were drowning in them.

"I think . . ."

Then a door slammed sharply behind them and footsteps were heard clumping up the for'ard stairs toward the deck.

Quint burst into view, his face diffused with red, his breath wheezing in his throat. His eyes looked eerily silver-blue in the half-light.

"Jo! Norm! Thank God I found you! We thought . . ."

"What's happened?" The moment between them was lost, as Norman Switec walked toward Quint.

"There's been some sort of an accident." The young man paused to catch his breath. "Watson Wise. He's missing. And we found that crazy saber we were playing with when he was dressed like Blackbeard. Also some burnt matches on the lower deck toward the stern. We think . . . he may have fallen overboard. He . . . he may even be dead."

Chapter Eight

All's fair in love and war.
—Shakespeare

They gathered in the Romanov salon on the dive boat, all of them except for Watson Wise, the snail expert, who was missing. It was a quiet and very somber group of people: the divers, the publicity people, Glen Howard, Norm, and Jo.

"I don't remember seeing him leave," Quint mumbled for the sixth time. "I mean, we were fooling around and he had the black wig that made him look like Blackbeard. And he lit those matches, of course."

"I can't think of why we thought it was so funny." Janna Lawrence was ensconced in one of the high-backed chairs, a blanket over her legs, chills wracking her body. Glen Howard hovered close, a glass of scotch in his hand.

"Here. Try this. That wine you've been drinking wasn't made to help in this sort of situation."

"I wonder what made him the expert." Norm Switec was speaking to Jo, but his voice carried across to the group of people gathered by the fireplace at the far end of the room. It wasn't cold, but everyone looked like they had a case of the chills.

Jo saw Glen's face tighten. "Good for you, Norm," she muttered out of the corner of her mouth.

"But he was so . . . inebriated," Dr. Smita Baid added. "Maybe he's just curled up someplace sleeping it off."

"The guy was just plain stinking drunk. Why not call a spade a spade?" Rocky Coke, one of the divers, stated bluntly.

Dr. Baid closed her eyes wearily. "The point is, maybe we should search the dive boat. There's no point expecting the worst."

"Captain Hornos and two other divers are checking," Glen Howard said softly. "But . . . I told him to go ahead and radio for the police. That sword and the matches. Wise was drunk. It's possible he was outside for some air and tumbled overboard. It could have been an accident."

Dr. Baid gave a jerky nod.

"But suppose it wasn't?" Quint put in.

All eyes were suddenly upon the young diver. "I mean, Watson was an expert swimmer. You wouldn't think it to look at him. If he'd just tumbled overboard . . ."

"Are you seriously suggesting that somebody here helped him along?" Glen Howard's voice registered incredulity. "But why? Who would want to kill a snail expert?"

"Why would anyone want to kill anyone?" Norman Switec added quietly. His eyes narrowed as he studied Glen Howard.

"Let's not jump to any conclusions. That's why we need the police," Dr. Baid added pointedly, looking at Quint.

Jo eased herself out of the group. Norman Switec turned and silently watched her depart for the Empress Room.

Once inside, Jo splashed cold water on her pale face. Her dark eyes looked shadowed with something more than shock. *Watson Wise.* It was hard to fathom that the drunk, little, round-figured man with the fake beard and fake sword might be permanently gone beneath the dark, treacherous waters.

She heard a clunk on the far side of the cabin. Jo peered out of the oversized porthole. The view was mainly of an ocean that had turned from an incandescent blue to a soulless black. Not even the little wavelets broke the surface of the sea. Then she saw the police patrol boat, a black and gray, twenty-one foot motor-driven launch. The bow cut like a sword through the black depths, followed by a lacy foam wake that reminded Jo of the layers of an old-fashioned petticoat.

She slipped back out into the passageway and returned to the main salon. Two men were down at the far end of the room, flanked by Glen Howard on one side, and the group from dinner on the other. The two men had just introduced themselves as Detective Jack Wolfe and Officer Campbell.

Wolfe was tall and overly thin, and reminded Jo of Icabod Crane in Washington Irving's ghostly Halloween tale. His eyes were those of a predator; there was a stillness about them, the color of cold, blue, gun metal. The tension in his lanky frame reminded her of a spring waiting to be released into action, police action. He surveyed the group in front of him, taking in the obvious nervousness of the women; the evasiveness of the men. Jo was reminded of a barracuda bearing down on a guppie for dinner, or guppies, as the case might be. She shivered suddenly and turned to the man standing at Wolfe's left.

Officer Campbell seemed the direct opposite of his superior, effecting almost a Laurel and Hardy contrast. He was small, muscular, and had a round, cherubic face and a notepad in his hands. His hair was longish—almost a Prince Valiant type of cut—and his eyes were a deep blue. They were watchful too. Wolfe and Campbell made a good team; what one missed the other would be sure to pick up and run with. The two men were shrewdly observing the group in front of them.

"Now you said, Mr. Howard, that Mr . . . er . . . Watson Wise disappeared after dinner. That he had had too much to drink and after playing as . . . er . . . Blackbeard with a fake beard and sword, he went up on deck."

"We assume he did, although I don't personally remember seeing him leave."

"All right. Officer Campbell is going to arrange to have the ship methodically searched, assuming Mr. Wise was inebriated and slipped off somewhere. Meanwhile, I would like to talk to each of you, individually. I gather," he turned to Captain Hornos, "there is a room available here?"

"The research library. It would be the best place. Quiet and private. Isn't that right, Norm?" The captain turned to the research librarian.

"It would be perfect."

Jack Wolfe continued speaking. "And if you'll return to your cabins afterward . . ."

"Are we under some kind of arrest? Because I, for one, never saw that little snail-hunter before I met him at dinner," Janna Lawrence declared. Jo saw her curl her fingers through her long blond hair, over and over again, almost like a nervous twitch that couldn't be controlled.

"Of course you're not under arrest. Or under any obligation to speak with me, at least for the present. I just assumed you would want to aid in the investigation of what's happened. For all we know, it could have just been an unfortunate accident."

There was a low murmur of agreement with Wolfe's words.

"Now, if Mr. Switec could direct me to the library . . ."

Jo saw the two men disappear out of the salon and go down a corridor toward the stern of the ship. Officer Campbell had discreetly departed sometime during Wolfe's speech, presumably to mount the diving operation. Jo looked across the salon at Glen. He appeared to be making his way toward her.

Jo turned hastily and found Dr. Baid curled up on one of the red and black chairs, her long legs tucked under her. The woman gave a welcoming smile as Jo collapsed on a nearby divan. Captain Hornos arrived with two glasses of scotch from the bar.

He was shaking his head. "Such an unfortunate occurrence."

Jo watched Glen Howard stop, hesitate, and then turn back to talk to Janna Lawrence, who was ensconced by the fireplace, Quint close at hand. Jo shrugged and tried to concentrate on what the captain was saying.

"Ah, here is Detective Wolfe back already. I will go

ahead and talk to him, since I really don't know anything about this Watson Wise."

The captain retreated down the corridor and out of the salon. Jo wearily leaned her head back and waited for someone to fetch her for the inquisition.

It appeared that Detective Wolfe was in no hurry to speak to her. The interviews dragged on. Jo was the last to be summoned by Officer Campbell, who seemed to have finished organizing the hunt for Watson on the ship. As the young man beckoned her in, Jo wondered again about the snail expert.

She seated herself across from Detective Wolfe at one of the teak tables in the library. The place was exactly as before, except that the vast computer screens were off and the outside lights had been dimmed. An overhead Tiffany-style glass lamp illuminated her face as she slipped into the chair. Detective Wolfe's face remained in half-shadow as he carefully studied her profile.

"Thank you for seeing me, Mrs. Howard."

"Sharpe. My name is Josephine Sharpe. Glen and I are in the process of getting a divorce." Jo thought again of the papers that still remained back at the Learned Owls and bit her lip. This trip could have been a golden opportunity, if only she had known Glen was going to be here.

Detective Wolfe began again. "We're still searching the ship for Watson Wise. I'm just trying to cover all the bases, so to speak. We'll probably have more information by the morning."

Jo tried to concentrate on what the man was saying.

"I see. Tell me, Detective Wolfe, was there any indication that anything has actually happened to the man? After all, he was very drunk."

"We're working on it, Ms. Sharpe. Interesting that your husband, er . . . ex-husband," Wolfe paused, "Er . . . Glen Howard asked the same question."

"Great minds, Detective, and all that." Jo winced inwardly. Trust Glen to come up with the same idea. Unfortunately, it would link the pair of them in Wolfe's mind.

"Had you ever met Mr. Wise before today?" Wolfe doodled with a pen, making little square boxes with circles around each one. Jo watched the repetition, fascinated.

"No. I came on board to do some diving on the *Queen Anne's Revenge*. Mr. Switec invited me. He works in the research library here. I met Mr. Wise for the first time at dinner this evening in the Romanov Salon." Josephine paused. "But surely you've discovered who did or did not know Watson Wise?'

"We're working on it, Ms. Sharpe." More doodles, these looked like birthday hats. Or perhaps they were dunce caps, Jo thought unkindly. A reflection of their maker, perhaps?

"We've talked to Dr. Baid, who was very friendly with Mr. Wise. They both follow the lecture circuit and are sponsored by the same college. She told me that they supplemented their incomes by speaking and writing. In Mr. Wise's case, the articles were on," and here he consulted his notebook, "multiple prey habits in community dynamics trait mediated effects of freshwater snails." Wolfe wrinkled his nose as if he smelled something bad. "Yet she and Mr. Howard mentioned that Mr. Wise seemed to be rather . . . er . . . flush with money. It seems he owned everything from . . ." back to the notebook again, "a townhouse on the Jersey Shore, a cherry-red Chevy Corvette, and a rare artwork called 'Nudes on Holiday.' Ms. Baid in particular had noted these possessions while working with Mr. Wise. She didn't have any explanation for where the money came from. Do you?"

Jo shifted uneasily. "Maybe he had a rich aunt? Or maybe the guy won the lottery? Did you consider that?"

"We're working on it, Ms. Sharpe. But . . ." and here Wolfe narrowed his eyes at her thoughtfully, "it could mean that he was blackmailing someone about something."

"Oh, come, Detective. The fellow probably just had a wealthy benefactor who likes snails. Did you consider that as a possibility? It doesn't necessarily have to be something illegal."

"It doesn't have to be, but often is. But we're working on it, Ms. Sharpe."

There was a long silence in the room. Wolfe doodled on.

Up on deck, Jo heard eight bells toll. Midnight. It was late indeed.

She shifted nervously. "Just what exactly are you suggesting, Detective?"

"It had occurred to me that perhaps your husband was Watson Wise's benefactor. Would you know anything about that?"

"Not a thing. Glen contributes to many noteworthy causes. It comes with the territory. I never heard anything about him supporting a snail expert. However, we have been separated for two years." She hesitated. "Although he's hardly the only wealthy philanthropist in New York. Have you checked out any of the others, Detective?"

"We're working on it, Ms. Sharpe. One last question. Would you mind recounting your movements right before you learned of the accident?"

"Not at all. I'd seen the whole group at dinner. Norm Switec and I met on the upper deck. And Quint was the one who came and told me about Watson Wise being missing and that the sword and matches from his beard were scattered around."

"In other words, you didn't see Glen Howard right before the accident?"

Jo thought back. She hesitated. The silence in the room deepened. Officer Campbell began to crack his knuckles. Jo gave him a look of annoyance.

"No. Not right before. But surely someone . . ."

"Unfortunately, a number of people seem to be unaccounted for."

"Glen has many faults, Detective, but believe me, pushing someone off a cruise ship isn't one of them. What about the other passengers and their movements?"

"We're working on it, Ms. Sharpe." He snapped the notebook shut, rather like in an old Columbo movie. She half expected him to say, "Now one more thing."

He didn't say it. As Jo rose, he followed her to the door.

"Are you going back to Beaufort, Detective? I saw the police cutter pull in and I was wondering if I could possibly

hitch a ride? I need to get back to my bookstore by tomorrow."

"Ah, yes, the Learned Owls. I don't see why not. We
really have no evidence of a crime. Officer Campbell will
probably discover Mr. Wise sleeping it off somewhere. Just
get down to the lower deck soon. I must get this evidence
processed." Wolfe paused. "If only you'll answer one more
question. I'm a bit puzzled, you see."

"Oh? And what exactly is puzzling you?"

"When I spoke to Mr. Howard, he er . . . didn't mention
anything about a divorce from you. I was wondering if you
had some explanation for that?"

Jo looked Wolfe over carefully. "It's like this, Detective.
We're working on it."

Jo hastened back down the companionway and charged
up the stairwell to her luxurious Victorian bedroom. After
tossing her belongings into a bag, she yanked the outside
door open, only to run straight into Glen.

"So you really are jumping ship, so to speak." He leaned
back against the door, as though he had all the time in the
world, which perhaps he did. "Are you that anxious to get
away from me?"

"Gee, you finally managed to figure that out? After all
this time?" Jo began edging through the door. The dark
mahogany wood scraped uncomfortably against her back.

"I thought . . . perhaps once we got back together . . ."

"We are not back together, Glen. There has been a separate you and a separate me now for two years, since I fell
and lost our baby. I'm not the same person anymore.
Maybe you don't understand, but I'm not. I need someone
I can depend on to show up and be there. You just never
seemed to fit the bill."

His face had whitened. "I came, you know. As fast as I
could get back from our Ho-Jo Publications London office.
I . . ."

"Please, Glen. Let's not rehash all this. It's over. I
thought we had both agreed. And especially now . . ."

"Why? What's happened now?"

"Detective Wolfe. He seems to think you may have been

black mailed by Watson Wise. It seems Watson spent far more money than he earned. And it would give you one hell of a good motive for murder."

"That snail expert? You honestly think I'd shove him overboard or some such?"

Jo sighed and shook her head. She half-turned and started to move down the corridor. "I don't know. Do you have an alibi?" Jo thought back to the dining table. "Were you with someone? Janna Lawrence, perhaps?" A petty tone had crept into her voice, but Jo was too tired to care.

"No, I wasn't with Janna, although it's interesting that you should think so." He stopped and ran a hand through his hair. "I really don't have an alibi at all, you see."

"What a shame. And too bad about Janna. She was always so conveniently around every other time, wasn't she, Glen? You told me everything was over and done with between the two of you when we got married. I used to wonder about that. I used to wonder a lot."

"You were always a little jealous of her, Jo. Although you have no reason to be."

"No. In order to be jealous, you have to care and I don't anymore. It's that simple."

Jo turned and walked slowly down the companionway. Glen caught up as they reached the bulkhead.

"Jo, wait! Don't go like this. Even if you still want a divorce, I care about you. I'd like us to try again. But regardless, I'm not sure it's safe. And you . . . you seem to draw the lightning, so to speak."

"The only thing I've noticed, the only time I haven't felt safe is right here and right now. With you." It wasn't really true, but Jo thought of the blond, blue-eyed Janna Lawrence. Suddenly she wanted to smash Glen's confidence. He thought he could just wave an arm and she would come running back. She'd prove him wrong, once and for all.

They were blocking the stairwell to the lower deck. As Jo turned to move past, a third figure joined them.

"Why don't you leave Jo alone? I don't think she particularly wants to talk to you, Howard!"

Glen turned to Norman Switec, whose head and shoulder had appeared over the stairwell. "I'm sure Josephine is capable of making up her own mind."

Jo looked from one man to another. Both were darkly furious and looked like they would need little excuse to charge each other. Blast it all anyway. She raised a hand.

"Glen, I'm leaving. I do want to get off the dive boat. Perhaps you're right. There have been a few too many accidents. And, if I don't go now, I'll miss my ride and be stuck until later."

"By all means, go then, Josephine. I wouldn't want you being stuck here."

The anger that had radiated from Glen Howard seemed to dissolve abruptly.

Norm took her arm.

"I'm really sorry it had to end like this, Glen. But things are better now. You'll see," Jo finished weakly.

"Better for who, Josephine? You, me, our baby?"

Jo stopped halfway down the stairs, her eyes haunted with unspeakable pain.

"I'm not sure, Glen. I just don't know anymore."

"Tell me if you ever figure it out." And he turned abruptly back down the companionway, leaving her alone with Norman Switec.

Chapter Nine

> And I watered it in fears,
> Night and morning with my tears;
> And I sunned it with smiles,
> And with soft deceitful wiles.
> —William Blake, *A Poison Tree*

"Whew! I'm sorry about that, Jo." Norman Switec had followed her down to the lower deck. "He's just so high-powered, so . . ."

"I understand. It's like Glen takes up all the air in the room, and there's never enough for anyone else. You're alive, but smothered."

"Yes. I suppose. Look, watch out for yourself. That's one thing Howard and I do agree on. It's not safe around here. I've felt something too."

Jo searched his face. "You don't think Watson's passed out somewhere or that he didn't just fall overboard," she murmured softly. "That's so, isn't it?"

Norman Switec nervously twisted his watchband around and around on his wrist. "I just don't know. There's a very strange feeling out here. Take care, Jo. Look, can I call you? Maybe we could get together for dinner. There's a restaurant out toward Wanchese on Roanoke Island, the Queen Anne's Revenge. They have fabulous food and," he paused unhappily, "maybe you'll have a better time than you had here."

Jo touched his arm. "I had a great time at the dive site. It wasn't your fault about Glen turning up. Or about Watson, either. And yes, I'd like to have dinner. Call me."

"Ms. Sharpe! We're ready to leave." Officer Campbell's almost boyish voice beckoned from over the gunwale. "If you're coming . . ."

Jo gave Norm's hand a squeeze and moved to the railing. She passed down the overnight case and then clambered into the police patrol boat. Campbell assisted her to a seat under cover of the wheelhouse before gunning the engine and pulling away from the dive boat.

Jo looked back. Norm waved once, but her attention was directed to a lone figure on the upper deck, watching her go. She somehow knew it was Glen. He hadn't gone back to Janna after all. Then the roof of the wheelhouse blocked both men from her view, as the cruiser turned back toward Beaufort.

The cruiser quickly reached the shore, where Officer Campbell secured the patrol boat to the pier. Detective Wolfe chattered in the back of the radio room. Jo grabbed her overnight case and ran for her car parked in the Beaufort Marina. It was obviously not a good time to linger, but she would have loved to discover what Detective Jack Wolfe was talking about. And with whom.

Jo yanked the Chevy's door open just as the clouds let loose with a curtain of rain. Tossing her bag in the back, she started the motor, stepped on the accelerator, and turned toward home.

By the time Jo pulled into the parking lot of the Learned Owls, the rain had ceased and the wind had stopped its devilish dance across the sand. The sky was turning a speckled melon color in the east as the sun's rays streaked upward and chased away the grayish-black of the night. Brown pelicans were diving for fish that the storm had brought to the surface. The air had the fresh salty tang Jo loved after a rainstorm.

She inserted her key into the lock and swung the door to the bookstore open. Flicking on the lights, she moved past Tara's place at the cash register. Her assistant wouldn't be in before nine, which would give Jo a chance to get a few hours sleep. Her eyes felt gritty with sand and her throat was parched. She half-stumbled through the store, dumping the overnight case on a bench before climbing the spiral staircase in the back to her apartment.

It felt good to be home, away from all the trouble on the dive ship. Jo wandered into the kitchen and put the water on for tea. The place had a deserted feel as though she had been gone for six months. And then it occurred to her that Marlowe had not come to greet her.

Jo frowned. Maybe he was sleeping in the bedroom and hadn't heard her. She eased herself out of the kitchen and back past the main room with the bronze lanterns over the fireplace. The dish of food was still sitting where she had left it, untouched, along with his water. Going through the arched doorway, Jo checked under the bed. Speckles of dirt met her gaze, but no Marlowe.

Relax, Jo told herself sternly. Maybe Tara decided to take him home for the night after all. But Jo's feeling of unease grew as she ran past the outer door and checked the stairs. Could he have somehow gotten outside? No, the door leading from the porch had been locked.

She turned back to the spiral stairs and hurried downstairs, pausing at the bottom of the steps to catch her breath. The bookshelves loomed around her—silent, mocking. It would be so easy for someone to be hiding, to leap out at her as she went past.

Then Jo heard the scratch, scratch coming from behind her. She turned and yanked open her office door. A tiger streak charged out, giving an exuberant yowl, and wound himself around Jo's legs.

"Marlowe!" Jo bent to scratch the dark head. "How did you get in there?"

She walked slowly toward her desk, running her hands over the surface. Had Tara forgotten and locked him in?

No, there was no food or water in the office and Marlowe had been in the store when she left.

The desk top seemed undisturbed and yet something was different.

Jo moved to the small safe against the far wall and snapped it open. Everything seemed to be in place. And yet she still felt that something was changed. The skin on the back of her hands began to crawl.

Marlowe jumped on the desk and daintily paraded across the surface. Jo turned back and tried the door. The knob was high up and the cat couldn't possibly have reached it, even it he could have somehow been able to jump the door. Jo clicked the lock back and forth; it held against her prying fingers.

There was only one way the cat could have gotten trapped in her office. Someone had been here, in the bookstore—searching. But for what? And when he had left, the cat must have slid inside and accidently been caught.

"What were they looking for, Marlowe?" Jo thought of the diary, hidden upstairs in the kitchen. She let the door bang as she bolted back into her apartment. The cookbooks were where she had left them, with a thin layer of dust on the covers. She yanked them down and pulled Betty Crocker open, half-expecting the diary to be gone.

The brown leather notebook was inside. Jo sat down at the kitchen table as Marlowe rushed over and began to gobble his breakfast. Her hands trembled as she opened the book and looked again at the quill pen writing on the page.

Jo shoved her short hair wearily back from her forehead. "I wish you could tell me, Marlowe; who was our visitor? Did they want money or this?"

But somehow Jo knew they had been after the diary. But who? Norman Switec had wanted to see it. But he thought she was bringing it down to the wreck site; he hadn't learned she hadn't brought it until later in the day. What about Glen? He couldn't have known about the diary, unless . . .

Jo thought of her young, dark-haired, impressionable assistant with her desire for happy endings. Could Tara have mentioned the diary to Glen? Had she gone looking for it and accidently locked Marlowe in?

Jo grasped the kitty and pulled him close. His pink tongue flashed out and he licked her hand, as though happy to be released from her office.

"I wish you could tell me what happened, little guy. Maybe I would have more of a clue as to what's going on around here."

The cat stared back at her and then began cleaning his fur. Jo's gaze dropped to the diary and Cristabel Lamonte's record of one of the most tragic events in her life. She glanced toward the bedroom; she had been tired, but now sleep seemed very far away.

"Someone broke in here because they wanted to see this, Marlowe. I think maybe it's time I sat down and read the whole thing."

Two hours later, Jo was still perusing the events leading up to Cristabel's kidnapping by Blackbeard. But now Jo read every word. A clue turned up in one of the sections where Jo had skipped ahead, where Cristabel spent her time talking about "Dear Papa" and her new stepmother. She also chattered on about her new cobweb-colored kitten, Chibbley, who spent hours playing with her knitting yarn.

Evidently a number of people had visited the Lamontes the following spring. Then Jo found the entry dated March, 1718, which made her forget her red eyes and tired back. As she read on she found Cristabel's enthusiasm contagious.

Our plantation has been honored with a visit from a gentlemanly pyrate named Stede Bonnet. He has been pardoned by the King's Governor, Mister Charles Eden, a most important man, in the city of Bath. Captain Bonnet has sailed south to Fishport and we received him recently. Papa had told me he was very learned, with great knowledge of medicine and such. While we were walking through the gardens, he encountered a shrub with three leaves, which he told me causes boils, pustules, and a rash all over the body.

Jo leaned back to rest her shoulders. It sounded like Cristabel's gentleman was talking about poison ivy. Jo read on.

Pyrate Bonnet tolde me of a tree native to his home in Barbados, an English island to the south, where sugar cane is grown. This tree when touched or even burned, causes sneezing, watery eyes, and blistering of the skin.

Barbados! Was that where the poison tree's name had come from? Norman Switec had mentioned that Blackbeard traveled all over the Caribbean, but perhaps he had never encountered this particular lethal tree and could have not realized the danger in burning the wood!

Cristabel rambled on about a great party being held for Captain Bonnet, but said nothing more about the tree.

Jo shut the diary. Where had Cristabel been when she was kidnapped by Blackbeard? Ocracoke? Or one of the other islands perhaps? On which island were the poisonous trees to be found? Jo yawned and rubbed her eyes thoughtfully, as she heard a car with a ragged motor pull into the car park below.

Jo eased down the spiral staircase, just as Tara bolted through the main doorway.

"Jo! You're back!" Her glasses slipped partway down her nose and her lipstick seemed smeared, as though she had been hurrying. Tara wore a chartreuse T-shirt, tie-dyed, with a picture of a yawning, striped kitten on the front. Dark blue shorts and sandals completed the outfit.

Suddenly Jo was very glad to see and hear another voice break the stillness of the bookstore.

"Where's Marlowe? I brought him some kitty treats."

Jo replied quietly, "Sleeping in my place upstairs. He somehow got stuck in my office last night." Looking at Tara's smiling, ever-so-normal expression, Jo began to have doubts about someone being in the bookstore. Perhaps Marlowe had managed to open and shut the door himself? her inner voice prompted. A strange chill crept over Jo; suddenly her hands felt clammy.

"So did you have a good time? And did you meet Quint? And did you dive the *Queen Anne's Revenge?*"

"Yes, to everything! Quint took me down to the wreck. But Tara, there was an accident." And in a few brief words, Jo told her assistant as much as she knew about what had happened to Watson Wise.

Tara leaned back in her chair, up against the window glass. The filtered sunlight turned her long dark hair into a gleaming satin cape that billowed around her slender shoulders. But her eyes had gone deadly blank, as though someone had shuttered them like a camera.

"You say this Watson Wise was a snail expert?" Tara trailed her finger over the desk, making an imaginary trail in the light.

"Uh-huh." Jo leaned back in one of the comfortable easy chairs by the coffee machine. "The police were still searching the dive boat when I left. Everyone seems to think that he went on a huge binge and was sleeping it off in some comfy corner somewhere." Jo studied the younger girl's face. "Why?"

"I knew a Watson Wise at the university. There was a rumor that, well, he was involved in dealing."

"You mean drugs?" Jo yanked herself erect. Her eyes, which had been half-closed were wide open.

"It was just a rumor. But he seemed to know an awful lot of the students, considering he was just a part-time teacher."

"We may never know now, one way or the other. But I'll call Detective Wolfe and mention it. It would certainly explain the man's income." Jo paused, biting her lower lip. The information would also help get Glen Howard off of the proverbial hook. Then she shook her head and changed the subject.

"I was reading Cristabel's diary when I got back. I finished it."

"What did you learn, then? Were there any more clues about the location of Blackbeard's treasure aside from that poison tree business?"

"I went back to when the family was living on the plantation. Cristabel talks about being visited by Stede Bonnet, another pirate, according to the expert, Norm Switec. Anyway, Bonnet mentions a poison tree in his native homeland, which was the island of Barbados." Jo hesitated. "I'm going to fly down there and investigate."

"But all that way? What do you expect to find?"

"I'm not sure exactly. But I've sort of run out of leads. The trail has gone cold except for Cristabel's poison tree. I think this is probably my last chance to find out what she meant."

"I'll take Marlowe home with me then. And don't worry. I'll mind the store."

"I know you will. I can fly down and back in a couple of days. As a matter of fact, I'll call Cyn and let her know where I'll be. Just in case she or Mother need me."

Tara leaned back in her chair, which wobbled dangerously on two legs. "I'll book you a flight on the Internet. And you can stay in one of those fancy hotels. There's bound to be some kind of package for a few days."

The chair clunked down as Tara began clicking information into a search engine. "Something with oleander-covered balconies and tall, dark, and handsome strangers lurking under every palm tree."

"Just try for one that won't drive me into bankruptcy," Jo observed drily. "I'll make do with it, handsome stranger or not!"

Later, Jo wandered back upstairs and dialed Cyn's New York number.

"Barbados?" Cyn's breathy, Lauren Bacall voice came on the line. "Oh, Jo! It's perfect timing! I'll fly down from New York and meet you! There's absolutely nothing, but nothing going on here. The opera is played out for the season and the new Broadway shows haven't started yet. And did I tell you about Eric?"

Eric? Jo's mind was still on pirates and Cristabel and Barbados. Who in the heck was Eric? Had she forgotten Cyn's latest trip to the altar?

"Eric," Cyn clarified a moment later, "has bailed out on

me for this vamp of a fashion model!" Cyn gave a disgusted sniff. "Younger men certainly aren't what they're cracked up to be. No loyalty, that's their trouble. They drop you at the first eye wrinkle that appears and move on to someone else."

"Gee, I can't imagine who that sounds like, Cyn. But are you sure you want to come? You can't swim and May will be hot like a furnace. You've said many times that the only use you have for water is taking a bath in it."

"True, true. I'll leave the swimming, diving, and so forth to energetic souls like you. So where are we staying?"

"I'm not sure. Tara's busy making the arrangements."

"Well, no matter. As long as it is big and expensive. I'll love it for sure. Just leave the name of the hotel on my e-mail."

"O.K. And Cyn, thanks for coming. It will be a lot more fun with you there."

"What are friends for, Jo? Oops, got to run. If I hurry, I'll have time to pick up one of those new bathing suits at Bloomingdale's. See you."

The dial tone sounded in Jo's ear as her friend hung up.

Jo paused only a moment and then dialed a second number.

Her mother's husky voice came over her answering machine. Jo rattled off a brief message about the trip she and Cyn had planned.

The last call was to Norman Switec, but he too seemed to be unavailable. Jo merely asked him to call. The man was possibly still out on the dive boat with the police, answering innumerable questions. It was hard to believe, but at this time twenty-four hours earlier, Jo had been on her way to the *Queen Anne's Revenge,* looking forward to diving again, convinced she wanted nothing more than a divorce from Glen Howard. Now everything had somehow gotten confused and changed and she no longer felt sure of anything.

Jo fished her passport out of the office safe and hid Cristabel's diary again within the cookbook cover. She was haphazardly throwing more clothes into her overnight case when the telephone shrilled in the upstairs bedroom.

Norm calling back so soon, Jo thought to herself, hastily picking up the receiver.

"I was hoping to catch you at home." The smooth, silky voice, which had always reminded her of James Mason, sounded in her ear. He could still send a pulse of anticipation up and down her spine.

"Hello, Glen. I wasn't expecting you to call." Jo dropped the black and white checked bathing suit she was holding into her bag.

"The police are still here on the dive boat. They came back again at morning's light. I gather they were going to start dragging the inlet for a body, but . . . Watson washed up on shore. No evidence of foul play. So the police are calling it a 'death by misadventure.' " He paused. "I guess after hearing that, I wanted to be sure you got back all right. I do worry about you, Josephine. It was quite a day for all of us."

"Thank you for checking." Jo heard her voice grow faint. It sounded to her like she was speaking from far away. She coughed and cleared her throat.

"Look, Josephine. I thought you would want to know. I'm—I've decided to give you what you want. I'm ready to sign the divorce papers. Just drop them in the mail."

Glen's voice had fallen to a harsh whisper at the end of his speech. It sounded strangely rehearsed.

"Why now, Glen? After all the hassle, why are you so willing to go along?"

"I guess I've finally concluded that there really isn't any point in going on with a marriage where both of us are so unhappy. After talking to you on the dive boat, I guess I realized that we'd done too much damage to each other to go back and fix things."

Jo pressed the receiver closer to her ear. "That sounds like Clark Gable's Rhett Butler speaking to Scarlett O'Hara in *Gone with the Wind.*"

"With one gigantic difference, my dear. She was the one

who didn't want to call it quits. And frankly, I never did believe that Scarlett got Rhett back, sequel or no sequel."

"Thank you, Glen. I truly think it's for the best."

"Do you? That's something I've finally done that meets your approval. If you'll just send the divorce papers, we can get this over with as painlessly as possible."

The receiver went dead in her ear. Jo stared for long moments at the telephone, as though it could answer the questions running through her mind.

She was free! He would sign the papers and their marriage would be over! It was what she had wanted him to do for months. And perhaps, eventually, she could forget the fall on the stairs that had resulted in her daughter's death.

"Are you all right, Jo? You look kind of funny." Tara Cataldo had come upstairs, quietly, to stand next to the desk.

"I'm fine. That was Glen. He's agreed to the divorce. At last."

"And are you happy?"

Jo laughed, but the sound had a shrill undertone to it. "Of course. Yes! I'm delighted!"

Tara gave Jo a quizzical look, turned, and slid back out of the room.

Jo put her head wearily down on the desk, as she suddenly realized that she wasn't really delighted about much of anything.

Chapter Ten

> Look like the innocent flower,
> But be the serpent under it.
> —Shakespeare, *Macbeth*

J o wearily dropped into the rear seat of a cab after clearing customs at Grantley Adams International Airport and leaned back in her seat as the driver loaded the overnight bag into the trunk. The flight had been far longer than she planned and had left her drained and exhausted. Tara Cataldo had made reservations for the weekend package at the Palm Terrace Hotel, a beautiful resort on the western side of Barbados, complete with tennis, golf, a restaurant, and a shimmering golden-yellow beach. Unfortunately, Cyn had managed to miss the flight out of New York and would be arriving the next day. So Jo was on her own for the first night.

Michael, the young black driver from the hotel, gave her a dazzling, brilliant smile. He edged the Mercedes cab into heavy traffic, driving on the left-hand side of the road as they cruised slowly toward the hotel. The cab made a half-circle as the driver carefully maneuvered through the British-style roundabout and kept on going. They passed a sign pointing to Sunbury Plantation, one of the historic manor houses found on the island, built when sugar cane was king and the wealthy lived like lords and ladies in exclusive luxury.

Was that the life that Stede Bonnet had left before he became a pirate and joined up with Blackbeard? For a man who knew next to nothing about sailing, the whole idea was incredible. Yet he had changed, according to the stories, from a wealthy, respected planter into a bloodthirsty ruffian on the high seas.

The cab crept slowly along from Christ Church to St. Michael's Parish and out to the coast. Traffic became lighter as they sped north toward the hotel, up what the locals called the "Platinum Coast."

The Mercedes sped past fields of cane outside. Then they were in Holetown, the major resort city on the west side of the island.

The houses here were brightly-colored reds, blues, pinks, and yellows, and were well-kempt with flowering flame-red poinciana and sun-colored begonias in every yard. Tourists flocked to the shops, which provided T-shirts, shells, groceries, and even a pirate cruise called the Jolly Roger. The two-lane road narrowed again before the driver pulled past a brilliantly white gate house, down an avenue of royal palm trees, and into the courtyard of the Palm Terrace Hotel.

The lobby was spacious and had a gigantic water fountain with red and black tropical fish darting to and fro. A painting of the local Bajan Market by Vonita Comissiong hung behind the main reception desk. Check-in was painless and Jo found herself, complete with a map of the grounds, being escorted by the hotel manager to her suite on the second floor.

The elevator was out of order, a fact for which the manager apologized profusely. It was sitting on the ground floor with a charred piece of the old-fashioned mechanism sticking out of the side. But the stone steps leading to the second floor were wide and easy to manage. Jo and her luggage were comfortably situated high above a double swimming pool with the ocean in the background below.

Finally everyone was gone and Jo had a chance to examine the beautiful room. The furniture was white wicker with bright parrot-colored bedspreads. Pictures of the famous green monkeys of Barbados hung over the two double beds. Jo trailed past the bath to the sitting room, where the island newspaper, *The Barbados Daily Nation*, had been left on the coffee table. A smallish kitchen, complete with flowered native pottery dishes, was on one side, while on the other was a library, complete with English, German, and French-language books. Jo moved across the dark tile flooring and out onto the balcony. A tiny green lizard saw her coming and scurried along the railing to disappear inside a leafy miniature palm.

If the suite was beautiful, the beach area was gorgeous. A swimming area with two pools was spread out below. The white stucco bungalows were like a frame for the warm yellow sand and the bluish-green, satiny water beyond. A diving platform had been set up and some hotel guests were splashing around close to the ladder. The Piperade Restaurant overlooked the shoreline with tables covered by brightly colored umbrellas. To the far left of the picture was a white, two-story plantation home, probably where the owner dwelt when he was in residence. Sunning herself by the side of the pool and looking completely at home was a white and brown cat, obviously a Devon Rex.

Jo moved away from the balcony and back into the cool, semi-darkness of the room. Pirates and poison trees. Both seemed completely out of place on this enchanted isle. And where should she begin looking in the few hours of daylight that were left?

Jo reflected back on Cristabel Lamonte's diary. The girl had spoken of the poison trees as being close to Blackbeard's campfire on the beach. Could she assume that that was their natural habitat? If such were the case, then perhaps the beach was where she should start.

Wearing the black-skirted bathing suit she'd bought at Sak's the summer before, Jo collected towels and shoes and made her way down the graveled path. A gardener wearing the blue and white uniform of the hotel staff was clipping at the sulfur-yellow begonia bushes that trailed along the sides of the pools. He looked up as Jo went past, headed toward the restaurant and the beach. The sun glistened off the scorching hot sand, while overhead, puffy, white clouds rippled across the heavenly blue of the sky. The route south was blocked by the rocky, isolated border of the beach house, so Jo turned north, trudging past the oceanfront suites of the Palm Terrace and over a stone perimeter. On the far side were the more colorful houses of the local residents. As Jo hesitated, trying to determine if she would be trespassing, a small, childish voice piped up directly behind her.

"Hey, lady from the hotel. Are you interested in seeing Hawksbill tortoises native to Barbados out in Mullins Bay? Fantastic sight, lady."

Jo turned. A thin, dark-skinned boy, wearing a hotel uniform was staring hopefully into her face.

"And how would we get out there?"

The boy turned. Jo gasped as she saw the misshapen hump across his shoulders that the loose white shirt was unable to conceal. The word *hunchback* shot, unbidden, through her mind. The hump made the boy's neck look short, smaller than normal; it was almost as if his neck was attached back between his shoulder blades.

"We can go on that, my jet ski. I work for the hotel. You can sign up at the desk."

Jo yanked her eyes away from his deformed back to look where he pointed. There was a hut down the beach with the hotel name painted in bright letters. They offered jet ski rides.

"How much?"

"Fifty dollars. American," the child responded.

Jo hesitated. She had the money in the coin purse she wore attached to her wrist. Yet she was hunting for poison trees and pirates, especially Stede Bonnet. She was hesitant to waste precious time on a joyride. Sympathy for the child won out.

"All right." Jo remembered she didn't know the boy's name. "I'm Jo. And your name is . . ."

A smile radiated across his face, creeping into his black eyes. "Turtle Pilgrim," he said and held out a hand. "It's actually Tyrone," he added confidentially, "but nobody calls me that. I am called Turtle by everyone because I take the tourists out into the bay to see the Hawksbills."

Jo solemnly shook the boy's hand. She had been afraid he had acquired the nickname because of the misshapen hump on his back. Children could frequently be unkind to one another. She vaguely remembered Cyn calling her "giraffe legs" at some point in the distant past. Jo had hidden behind pants and long skirts because of it for years.

The boy took the money, jammed it into his shirt pocket, and then helped Jo onto the jet ski.

"You would like to ride in front and steer?" he asked anxiously. "Yes." Jo had done this before with Glen in happier days on Ocracoke. As Turtle started the motor, he clambered on behind her. She eased the jet ski away from the dock and out into the glistening water.

The boy pointed to the right, up the coast and away from Palm Terrace. Jo slammed into the incoming waves before she got the hang of hitting the water sideways. Glancing back, she saw the gardener shading his eyes, clipped bushes forgotten, as she and Turtle pulled farther out into deep water.

"Faster, faster," the boy yelled.

Jo pressed down on the throttle and the motor gave a loud roar. The coast, with its colorful houses, the palm trees, and the other tourists on the beach spun past. A small, local church with a golden cross on the cupola disappeared from sight. As Jo followed the coast north, the current changed direction; suddenly the waves and foam were splashing across the front of the jet ski and onto its passengers. Jo slowed down, fearful of overturning.

"Whee! Why you stop, Jo? This is great fun!" Turtle chortled from the back.

"Right. Great fun." Jo clamped her hand over the accelerator on the handlebars. Turtle pointed ahead; a group of small boats were huddled in a circle. People were peering over the side into the water.

"There they are! The Hawksbills! Other tourists are looking too!"

Jo eased the jet ski closer and joined the group, which seemed to be in a flux of movement. There were two other jet skis, several sloops, and a small cabin cruiser. Everyone was looking down while maneuvering constantly for a better position. It reminded Jo of the old television Westerns, when the wagon master would circle up the wagons for protection against wolves and Indians.

"Look, look!" Turtle chortled and pointed downward. "There is Big Bamba now."

Jo peered into the emerald-green depths. The water had an almost purplish cast farther down. She saw several huge shadows, gliding ever so silently; shells blending into the bottom of the bay. The tortoises seemed to be feeding on something far below. Silver-scaled fish darted in and out among the creeping giants.

Jo circled the jet ski slowly. The huge creatures seemed completely unaware of their audience. They were either very interested in their food or had become immune to the visitors due to constant contact.

"Tortoises are protected now in Barbados. Like a . . ." the boy paused, searching for the correct word, "a sanctuary, so that they cannot be harmed."

Jo thought of how cumbersome and awkward the tortoises were on land and how they glided and frolicked in the water, in their element.

"They belong out here. This is where they are happy," she said.

"Only lay eggs and have young on the shore," Turtle explained slowly.

Jo finally turned away. The group of tortoise-watchers started to break up. First the cruiser backed off and then two of the sloops. Jo aimed the jet ski south, past the rows of pastel houses and toward Palm Terrace.

The waves were a bit higher and foamed white over the jet ski. Turtle laughed and Jo laughed with him. She swung into the small pier and ran the machine into the beach, before killing the motor.

"You have a good time, Jo?" Turtle asked anxiously. Jo had the feeling that it really mattered to the boy that she had enjoyed herself.

"Yes, Turtle. Tell me, do you know anything about the pirates that used to roam the shores of Barbados? Where they came from, especially?"

Turtle's face scrunched up as he thought. "I do not know," he said slowly, "but my mother might. Her name is Annie. She knows the legends. Our family has been on this island a long time. Perhaps she could tell you."

Jo dismounted off the jet ski. "Is she home now, Turtle? When could I speak with her?"

"Not now. She works cooking in a restaurant down in Bridgetown." Turtle brightened. "But tomorrow, she will be home. It is Saturday." He looked at Jo appraisingly. "She can tell you about pirates. Also, my mother can tell fortunes. Using cards or the crystal or palms. You like your fortune told too, Jo? Only fifty dollars!"

It seemed to be the standard price, at least as far as Turtle was concerned. "No fortune, Turtle. But I might be interested in information. Not just about pirates, but about a kind of tree. A poison tree. Have you ever heard of it?"

Turtle wrinkled up his nose. "No tree that I know of is called this. But my mother will tell you. Perhaps to the north or on the other side of the island. This I do not know."

"I will be glad to pay for the information. Naturally."

Turtle smiled a wide, angelic smile. "My mother say I am good for making money. She says I am an . . ."

Hustler? The word shot through Jo's mind.

"Entrepreneur," Turtle finished proudly. "You come at ten o'clock." He gestured toward the bright blue cottage where he lived. "My mother will tell you everything you would want to know. And then some."

The boy grinned before turning and trotting up the path to his home, as Jo made her way slowly back down the beach to the hotel.

* * *

The gardener was still hacking away at the begonia bushes as she passed him on her way to her suite. Jo could feel his eyes boring into her back. She paused at the edge of the pool to peer around at him. Several other guests were lounging in the late afternoon sun. Nobody seemed to be paying much attention to anything.

Jo shrugged and ambled up the graveled path. White pigeons flapped suddenly up from one of the poinciana trees bordering the building. The tenant in the suite below Jo's gave her a friendly wave as she went past. Jo slid into the inside patio. The elevator was working and clinked noisily up to the second floor.

The answering machine blinked like a red, evil eye. The message from Cyn was short and direct: the plane had had engine trouble, and due to an unscheduled stop, wouldn't be arriving before late tomorrow. Disappointed, but looking forward to the next day's events, Jo thoughtfully looked over the stucco balcony to the beach house beyond. The plantation home remained dark and deserted. The trees above the front entranceway were guarded by griffins, half-eagle and half-lion statues, with wings and tails. Jo wondered again about the people who lived there.

Suddenly she felt exhausted. The long flight and lack of sleep on the dive boat seemed to have caught up with her all at once.

"I'll lay down for a minute and then go down to the Piperade Restaurant for dinner," Jo murmured to herself. There was a limbo dancing show later, but she needed to lie down for just a moment.

It was her last conscious thought before the brilliant sun streamed through the shutters the next morning.

Chapter Eleven

And it grew both day and night,
Till it bore an apple bright.
And my foe beheld it shine.
And he knew that it was mine.
　　　—William Blake, *The Poison Tree*

The sun glowed a sultry orange over the beach at the Palm Terrace the next morning. Jo took the elevator down to the first floor and crossed through the elaborate begonia garden toward the main lobby. High overhead the palm trees rustled as tiny green monkeys swayed and dived, almost like birds, from one branch to another. The Devon Rex cat was in residence once more, sitting alongside the griffins which guarded the path to the plantation house overlooking the beach.

Jo paused next to the sprinkling fountain and stared at the two picture windows of the beach house. They conjured images of malevolent eyes peering out at any of the travelers who crossed their path. But the heavy brocade draperies remained drawn against the shafts of morning light peeking through the heavy shrubbery, dividing the place from the rest of the hotel.

The lobby was cool and refreshing with the air conditioner running full blast. Jo stopped at the desk; a young black woman, dressed elegantly in the hotel's blue and white uniform, approached with a smile. Her name badge identified her as Octavia Dodd.

"Ms. Sharpe! I hope you have recovered from your exhausting trip yesterday." The woman's voice had a warm, lilting quality to it, almost like that of a singer.

"Yes. I wanted to tell you how much I enjoyed the room. I have a friend, Cynthia Savene, who will be arriving later today. Just in case I'm not back yet."

"We have her registration card right here. Such a shame her plane was delayed."

"I was looking at the plantation house down toward the beach. It seems so deserted." Jo let a questioning tone creep into her voice.

Octavia responded. "The rich and the famous. They winter here and summer farther north." The woman noted Jo's interest and continued. "We have many celebrities who come to our island. The late Princess Margaret had a villa and spent several months right on this coast every year. Plus we have the usual run of big name stars. Sir Anthony Hopkins paid us a visit a while back. Of course, many of the most famous wish to remain anonymous. We try and respect that under all conditions."

"Thank you for the information. And I'll try not to stare if I run into any celebrities." Jo let her sentence end in another question, but hotel employees had definitely been told to respect the privacy of the guests. Octavia merely smiled and turned back to her computer as Jo ambled past the gift shop and exercise rooms and out onto the driveway.

She trailed down the road, the palm trees swaying above in the salt-scented breeze. Turning left, Jo followed the walkway up to the door of the bright blue house. A sign in the window proclaimed this to be the home of the tarot reader. It was precisely ten o'clock when she rapped sharply with the wooden knocker on the door.

There was a sound of scurrying feet as the door was thrown open by Turtle. His face broke into a happy smile. The boy wore a T-shirt with a Nascar picture on it and the same pair of Bermuda shorts as yesterday.

"You came, Jo!" He held open the door and motioned for her to enter.

"Turtle? Is that our guest?" The voice was soft with a quiet elegance. The owner of the voice stood with her back against the shafts of light creeping through draperies at an enormous bay window.

Turtle's mother came forward, holding out her hand. She moved lightly and seemed to float across the room. Annie Pilgrim had the sort of appearance that the eye would slide across, but then double back for a second look. Her eyes were charcoal-colored and her face was framed by dark hair hanging straight down her back. She wore a rather shapeless house dress, but when Jo looked into her face, the sympathy and kindness made all the rest of no importance.

The hand she placed into Jo's was roughened and the nails short with no polish. Jo sank down quietly onto the light colored bamboo sofa, amidst soft, colorful cushions.

"You must be Jo. Turtle has told me that you are interested in the pirates of Barbados. Also," and here a question crept into Annie Pilgrim's voice, "a kind of tree. A poison tree?"

"Yes. It probably sounds strange." With no prompting, Jo briefly explained about Cristabel's diary.

Annie steepled her hands on her lap before turning to her son. Turtle had remained hovering by the door, as though uncertain whether to go or stay.

"Turtle, why don't you put the tea water on for Jo. This could take some time."

The boy nodded silently and left. Jo could hear him moments later banging around in the kitchen.

"He's a nice boy. You must be very proud of him."

The woman nodded. A smile curled her lips. "Yes. Turtle works hard and he is bright in school. But . . . ." here Annie paused, "you have seen his back. It is deformed and will continue to get worse. The other children make fun of him at school. They call him the snapping tortoise because of this disease in his spine. It is . . . scoliosis, I think the local doctor said."

"But can't anything be done? To straighten his spine, I mean?"

"There is an operation, but he would perhaps have to go to England or the United States. It costs a great deal of money. And Turtle must have it soon. The longer he has to wait, the more of a curvature there will be."

Annie fell silent as Turtle returned, bearing a tray with cups of Earl Grey tea and small brown cakes. He placed these on the tamarind table in front of the women and went to huddle by the door.

"But you wished to hear of the pirates. Pirate, I should say. Barbados only has one who came from the island. Although many of them stopped here on their travels around the Caribbean. This island, when it was first settled by the English, was noted for sugar cane. The sugar cane was made into rum. So of course the pirates came. They were all great drinkers in those days."

"And this pirate's name? From Barbados?"

"Stede Bonnet. It's odd, in a way." Annie Pilgrim turned her teacup slowly around in her fingers. "He had everything to make him happy. At least outwardly. The English had settled Barbados much earlier. Holetown was the first permanent settlement. By the time Stede "came out" as they say in England, the island had a booming economy because of the sugar cane being turned into alcohol. There are still factories that do this in the central part of Barbados. Stede owned a plantation close to Upton, but he and his wife and children lived in the capital, Bridgetown. They had all the outward signs of prosperity, including, of course, Stede Bonnet's position in society. He had served in the army and had the rank of major. He was also a justice of the peace, aside from owning Upton Plantation. But he spent a lot of his time in Bridgetown, where the pirates hung out, mainly in the taverns. Anyway, at the age of twenty-eight, Stede up and decided he wanted to become a pirate."

"I had heard his wife might have had something to do with it," Jo interjected delicately.

"That could have been true. Mrs. Bonnet was rather . . . er . . . bellicose. In addition to screaming at her husband, she threw dishes at him and literally shut the man out of the house. It's tragic. He was so afraid of her that after he was captured, much later in Charleston, he requested to be buried in the marshes outside of the city, presumably so she would never find his grave. And this from a man who had his captives walking the plank!"

"Walking the plank? I thought that was merely a legend from Walt Disney's Captain Hook in *Peter Pan.*"

"It was, for the most part. Very few pirates were so blood-thirsty. Stede Bonnet turned out to be the exception, though. Anyway, he sailed off in a ship that he had purchased to face doom and disaster in the Carolina Capes. He ended up being captured and hanged."

"And that was the end of him, then?"

"Completely. The plantation is gone. Of course, he never came back to Barbados."

"Tell me, Annie. Is there a tree on this island that is called a poison tree? Cristabel's diary mentioned it, along with Stede Bonnet being a guest at their plantation outside of Fishport. I gather Cristabel was rather taken with him."

"Oh, he was charming with the ladies, although he lacked skills for pirating. Anyway, there is a tree on Barbados that could be called such. It drips a sap that scalds the skin and blisters anything it touches. I suppose," and here Annie paused, "it might be called a poison tree."

"And Stede would have known of it?"

"Most definitely. The tree grows all over the island, but especially just north of here, about half a mile past St. Francis Church. You could walk to this place if you wish. The tree is called the machineel and is marked by red paint."

"I'll need to go up there."

Annie slowly drew a piece of writing paper from the table toward her. "I will make you a map. I grew up in the north coast area. I know it like the proverbial back of my hand."

Annie drew rapidly. "But you must not get too close and under no circumstances should you touch the fruit."

She handed the map to Jo, who stared down at it thoughtfully.

"It seems easy enough. I'll try my luck tomorrow." She rose and held out a hand.

Annie shook hands firmly as Jo continued.

"And thank you so much. I have just one more question about these trees. Are they native to just Barbados?"

"Oh, no. But Barbados seems to have been blessed, or perhaps cursed, with an abundance of them. The trees grow by the water, so many were cleared out of the forest areas on the west coast. But they are the only serpent, so to speak, in the Garden of Eden. And the trees range all the way into your own country, in the areas of Florida and even farther north."

"So it is possible they may have been found in North Carolina?"

Annie wrinkled her nose. "Perhaps. Who can say where the winds and birds transport seeds? But surely there is something more I can do for you? You paid Turtle fifty dollars. It is his standard rate for all tourists, but I feel you are being cheated. What about a tarot reading with the cards? I am very skilled. Or with the crystal if you prefer? When you came in, I felt for a moment you had a sadness in your soul."

Jo explained bluntly, "I have a stinker of a husband, is all. And I'm not sure what to do about him." She dropped her head and carefully placed the map in her purse. "And I certainly wasn't cheated." Jo smiled warmly. "Believe me, not in the slightest. You've helped me more than you will ever know!"

It was early afternoon when Jo emerged from the bright blue house and wandered back to the Palm Terrace Hotel. The sky overhead was filled with rippling cirrus clouds, which Jo fancifully thought looked rather like the scales on fish. She glanced down toward the beach; the miniscule waves whispered up toward the shore, while in the high begonia bushes, finches trilled.

Jo saw Turtle taking another tourist aboard his jet ski for a visit to the tortoises. She waved before turning into the long palm-decked driveway leading into the hotel. After collecting her key at the front desk from the ever helpful, gracious, and smiling Octavia Dodd, Jo rode the clanking elevator back to her suite. Cyn was still in route, so she picked up the telephone and called Norman Switec at the Currituck Aquarium. He answered on the second ring.

"Jo! Great to hear from you! The police just left. They've been around asking more questions about Watson Wise. It seems like the man has become far more important in death than he ever was in life."

Jo grimaced. It felt like the *Queen Anne's Revenge* and the death of the snail expert had taken place in another world, in a different life. It was completely removed from where she was now.

"So how are things going?"

"Fine, Norm. It's beautiful here and I think I may have a lead on the poison tree location that Cristabel talked about in her diary."

There was a long, drawn out silence at the other end of the line. "You mean . . . you may have a location for the treasure?"

"I wouldn't put it quite like that. And I don't want to sound too hopeful. Look, why don't we get together when I return? I'll tell you about it then."

"Fine, Jo. We can have dinner at this little restaurant I know out in Wanchese. You'll love it!"

Jo hung up seconds later. She frowned at the telephone, not actually seeing it. *Did* she have a lead as to the location of the treasure? Jo wasn't sure. She wandered over toward the balcony and leaned out. The stately palmetto trees made shadows of dark green and indigo, reflected in the pool. Two children were running around, screaming with excitement, while a middle-aged man, obviously a parent, looked on indulgently. A mottled lizard ran back and forth across the balcony railing as Jo turned toward the air conditioned interior.

Jo dropped down onto the comfy couch and propped her feet up on the bamboo coffee table. She flicked the switch on the remote control. A television program was just beginning. It was at the same moment, right on cue, that the key turned in the lock and a familiar, little-girl voice announced, "Jo! I'm here! At last!"

And Cynthia Savene walked into the room.

Chapter Twelve

Said the cunning Spider to the Fly:
'Dear friend, what can I do
To prove the warm affection I've always felt
for you?
 —Mary Howitt, *The Spider and the Fly*

Cyn walked in wearing a floral dress that looked rather plain, but in reality was likely very expensive. She surveyed the suite with a casual glance before turning to the dark-skinned young man hauling her bulging suitcase, who was sweating profusely in the heat.

"At least the room was worth waiting for." She indicated with a vague wave of her arm where the luggage was to be placed. An emerald and white diamond bracelet glittered on her right wrist.

Jo dragged herself erect. "I see you have a new decoration."

"Yes. I consoled myself for all the hassle and delays by having a looksee at some emerald emporium in Grantley-Adams Airport." Cyn pressed a bill into the young man's hand and waved him away.

Cyn wandered over, kicked off her pumps, and dropped into a chair. She yanked a poinciana flower from the vase and began methodically shredding it. The diamond bracelet glistened brilliantly even in the subdued light.

105

"So what have you been busy doing? Any luck with the treasure hunt?"

Jo outlined briefly what had occurred and told Cyn about Annie Pilgrim and her son. "I'm going to hike north tomorrow to search for the trees. Would you like to come along?" she added as an afterthought.

"Oh, dear me, no, darling. I'm going to soak up some sun on that snow white beach down there. They call this the Platinum Coast of the Caribbean. I plan to enjoy it, now that I've finally arrived. But you say this woman and the boy were so helpful. They seem to know quite a bit about pirate lore here on Barbados. Did you show them Cristabel's diary?"

"No. I left it at home." Jo bit her lip, thinking about Turtle Pilgrim. "The boy is a hunchback. Some sort of scoliosis of the spine. I wish there was something I could do. His mother works as a cook in a restaurant and tells fortunes on the side. She doesn't have the money for an expensive operation."

Cyn snorted. "And neither will you if you get a divorce from Glen. Honestly, Jo, if you're going to keep running around picking up strays, you'd better latch onto more money in a hurry! Alimony doesn't go as far these days as it used to, what with lawyers getting their share." Cyn turned from the wrecked flower to a bowl of fruit and began nibbling on some blue grapes.

"Turtle's not a stray, Cyn," Jo said quietly, her dark eyes beginning to smoulder. "They've just had some bad luck."

"Of course he's not; they never are. At least as far as you're concerned." Cyn continued snacking on the grapes. "At least the fruit here is decent. I couldn't eat any of the awful gook they served on the plane!"

"We can go down for dinner if you'd like. The Piperade Restaurant is right across from the beach house." Jo steepled her hands thoughtfully in front of her.

"Beach house?" Cyn jerked erect. "Is that the white, decked-out plantation mansion I saw coming in? With the funny little half-eagle, half-lion figures at the gate?"

"The griffins? Yes, that's it. Do you remember Glen ever

saying anything about owning property in Barbados? You
knew him before we were married."

Cyn's brows furled. "No. Never heard. But I never heard
he'd invested in treasure hunting on the *Queen Anne's Revenge,* either. When a guy is so rich he owns half of the
country in one way or another, who can say? He probably
doesn't recollect all of his investments!"

"Good point," Jo muttered, almost to herself. "Who can
say?"

Jo made her way back upstairs later that night. The elevator whispered and creaked and sounded like it was about
ready to breathe its last before stopping on the second floor.
Jo hoped it didn't expire before they left on Monday. It
would just add to the list of Cyn's complaints, which were
already the traditional mile long. Although her friend had
seemed to be having a good time with the sandy-haired
man they'd been drinking with at the Shell Bar after dinner.
Her face had eventually lost its bored, sullen expression
and was almost animated—with narrowed eyes the huntress
had moved in on the prey.

Jo watched the two of them. Cyn's new friend had an
Adam's apple that reminded her of a golf ball stuck in a
snake's throat. But perhaps she was being unkind. Besides,
the fellow could turn out to be Cyn's next husband, assuming his bank balance was big enough.

The maid from the hotel had been in and turned down
the two huge beds. She had also replaced the shredded
poincianas with tropical-colored orchids. Jo walked over
and peered across the balcony. The sunset was all gold and
indigo and amber, reflected in sparks of light off of the sea.
Below her, the music from the bar drifted up, wafting past
on the wind. The smell of the open-pit barbecue from dinner reached her nose. She half-turned away, glancing at the
palm-shrouded beach house with its griffins across the way.
The windows from the place still reminded her of malevolent eyes watching, always watching. Jo told herself not
to be fanciful, the green monkey pattering around outside
of her window had more of a personality than the house.

Jo moved restlessly through the suite and finally collapsed on the bed. Sleep seemed a long ways away, but she eventually dropped off into an uneasy doze, only to waken early with the sunlight making dappled shadows across the bed. Dragging herself upright, she checked Cyn's bed; her friend had not returned to the suite the night before.

Jo shrugged. Cyn was a big girl and more than capable of taking care of herself. She'd shown this over and over again. Jo put her friend out of her mind and got ready for the hike northward.

Jo glanced toward the balcony and the beach house again. In the daylight it was silent and deserted and no more sinister than any other plantation house on Barbados. The griffins appeared as harmless statues and stood silent guard under a sky filled with amethyst and gray clouds.

Jo rode the clanking elevator down to the front desk. The ever helpful Octavia handed her an envelope from Cyn. The message was short and sweet: "Whee! I'm having fun! Finally! See you later, C."

And to think I was worried! Jo left the coolness of the hotel and turned north, following the sidewalk past St. Francis Church. Tiny hummingbirds fluttered in the trees skirting one side of the road, while stately white coconut palms reigned on the other side.

Jo pulled out the map that Annie Pilgrim had given her the day before. She ran a finger down the sharp black line which represented the jagged coastline. According to the map, the stand of trees was located directly north and very close to the water. Jo turned left and followed a wooded path. The dense vegetation became even heavier. The elusive green monkeys chattered in the trees overhead, while flaming orange and blue bird of paradise bloomed below.

Jo stopped, pushing her short, dark hair back from her face. Despite the soft-scented breeze from the bay, the air was heavy with the almost sour smell of the lush vegetation. After walking a ways, she saw them—the grove of machineel trees—each marked with red paint so hopefully no unwary tourist would be accidently poisoned.

The trees were about thirty feet tall with the long, stalky

leaves forming a crown high above the earth. Edging closer, Jo spied the greenish round fruits scattered haphazardly around the base of the trees. These were what caused the blistering and the milky sap that, when burned, made the eyes sting and water.

The breeze was quiet and Jo could hear the hammering of her own heartbeat. She looked and saw the tiny green and brown orchids, but here, in what she considered to be a grove of evil, it seemed like the petals and pistils were tiny faces with mouths, opening and crying out in anguish. Across the far side of the glen were the orange and blue of the bird of paradise plants, but this bird had a devilishly sharp beak that Jo surmised could easily slash out an eye.

Jo backed farther away and warned herself again not to be so fanciful. These were just plants and trees like any other; larger perhaps, because of the warm, tropical climate of the island, but not that much different from plant life in North Carolina.

Then there was a rustling through the underbrush. The white egrets rose in a spiraling circle, high into the air, screaming like children in pain. Jo half-dropped to the woody floor of the glen. She heard the distinct plop of footsteps coming closer, as shoes made a squishing noise through the sand.

She spun away from the poisonous milksap of the machineel trees and from the frightening flowers with petals like the long tongues of green lizards, seeking to entrap an unwary victim. Jo pushed rapidly away through the underbrush, back toward the road and safety.

The footsteps followed. Jo huddled down closer to the ground. Gigantic, blue flies hovered over her head, while two little lizards fell from an overhanging branch down onto her hair, their suction-cupped feet grappling frantically for a hold.

Then Jo saw him, wearing the white duck trousers and tropical shirt so common in the Caribbean islands. The footsteps stopped as he turned. For a second, it seemed to Jo that he would go past, but he paused, spotted her, and swooped down rather like a bird of prey, pinning her against him.

"Why, Ms. Sharpe! Are you all right? Octavia saw you leave and sent me to help. She was afraid of some mishap."

Jo peered up into the dark, handsome face of Michael, her driver from the airport.

"Oh, Michael! I . . . er." What excuse could she give for crawling around in the brush like some insane woman? "I just . . ."

Miraculously, Michael seemed to understand. Or maybe because of his job at the Palm Terrace, he was used to dealing with batty Americans. Jo put her hand in his and let him help her onto her feet.

Michael glanced at the sun in the western sky. "We really should be getting back. There's a samba party with local Barbadian dishes at the hotel tonight. You don't want to miss it, your last night here."

The hotel. It seemed like another world. Jo glanced back at the machineel trees. They seemed to be huddled together, watching and conspiring against her as she followed Michael back toward the Palm Terrace Hotel. Her last glimpse back revealed a pair of eyes that seemed to peer out from the wrinkled bark of the trees. She shuddered and kept on walking hurriedly in her driver's wake.

The trip back didn't take long, but the sky was already alight with the amber, russet, and orange of a beautiful sunset when Michael left her on the other side of the white stucco gatehouse. Jo collected her key from Octavia at reception—*didn't the woman ever take a break?*—and was moving toward the outer door leading to the patio when she heard a familiar voice.

"Why Mrs . . . er . . . *Ms.* Sharpe!" Dr. Smita Baid was just returning her own key. The Indian woman was wearing a striking black-and-white bathing suit and had probably spent the day by the swimming pool.

"Dr. Baid! Imagine running into you again! And in Barbados of all places!"

Smita Baid smiled. "Actually I'm here for a conference in regard to ocean pollution. I decided to come at the last minute. Things were so depressing at the dive site on the *Queen Anne's Revenge* after the death of that poor little man, Watson Wise. I just had to get away."

"Enjoy your stay. I'm here with a friend, but we're leaving tomorrow. It's a beautiful island."

"So I've heard. Actually, I'm going to see some Hawksbill tortoises with a young man on a jet ski. A very enterprising young fellow!"

"You must mean Turtle. He does get around."

"I'll see you later. You're coming to the party?"

"Naturally. Wouldn't miss it. They're having native dancing right after dinner at eight."

Jo waved and turned aside. She could feel the doctor's eyes following her as she crossed the courtyard and made her way to the elevator and up to the suite. She eased the door open and promptly found a note from Cyn. Brief and to the point, it read. "Came and went. Will see you at the party! C."

Jo crumpled the note and wandered through the empty suite. The place was filled with a feeling of aloneness. Crossing out onto the balcony overlooking the light-shafted pool, Jo could see the ocean, dark except for the shadowed moon casting subtle webs across its surface. Below her, the Devon Rex cat stalked one of the tiny, green-spotted lizards, chasing its prey under a blossoming buttercup-yellow poinciana tree.

Jo turned suddenly away from the balcony. She yanked open the huge closet on one side of the suite and pulled out the flame-red evening gown hanging there. She could wear the dress tonight along with the thin-strapped sandals and get very, very drunk in the Shell Bar. Perhaps she could forget about Glen Howard, her dead baby, and her failed marriage for one evening. At least that was the plan.

Jo dressed slowly, not wanting to arrive early at the party. Music filtered up from the Piperade Restaurant, along with songs sung by a husky-voiced singer, who sounded rather like Lauren Bacall in *To Have and Have Not*. Only this wasn't Cuba, but Barbados, and Humphrey Bogart wasn't waiting for her down in the Shell Bar. Nobody really was waiting for her. Cyn would be off with her current love interest. Nobody would even notice if Jo didn't show up at all. The thought was infinitely depressing.

Jo turned back to the dresser and clipped long, dangling earrings on before checking the mirror one last time. Cinderella going to the ball, only there was no Prince Charming. Had there ever been for her? Jo couldn't be sure.

She collected her evening bag and edged toward the rickety elevator, balancing precariously on her gawky sandals. Perhaps the stairs would be better. But no, not in these shoes. Jo pressed the button and the hoist swinging the elevator came up to the second floor. The door slid open to blackness beyond. Jo moved to step into the elevator, but one of the sandals caught on the edge of the cement walk leading into the car. Jo's leg buckled under her and she fell heavily to the side. Her arm flayed down into the empty air of the elevator shaft where the car should have been. But there was no car, just the vacant space where Jo would have stepped and fallen. She pulled herself erect as the enormity of what had almost happened struck her with a chilling coldness. And then she began to shudder uncontrollably.

Chapter Thirteen

'Oh no, no,' said the little Fly,
'to ask me is in vain,
For who goes up your winding stair
can ne'er come down again.'
 —Mary Howitt, *The Spider and The Fly*

"**A**re you sure you're all right? My God, when I stop and think . . . you could have fallen down the shaft and broken your neck!" Cyn Savene paced back and forth. Even in anger, her movements seemed so smooth; she drifted across the room. "If I hadn't needed an aspirin and come back to the suite, you could have lain there for hours!" Cyn's flimsy dragon-cup, blue dress floated to and fro as she swiveled. "How could this have happened? Don't these elevators have regular maintenance?" Cyn half-snarled at the fourth person in the room, Octavia Dodd. Michael, Jo's driver, had mysteriously appeared from nowhere and hovered in the doorway.

Jo winced at Cyn's tone from her place on the bed, where she had staggered and collapsed after the accident. But Octavia didn't seem at all intimidated.

"Mrs. Savene, the elevator was just repaired. Of course we will look into this accident immediately. Michael," she waved a graceful hand at the young driver, "will go down

113

at once. Perhaps some malfunction? I don't really know yet. But it will be handled!"

"You're damned right it will be handled!" Cyn parodied Octavia's voice, "and right now! How does it go in these tropical backwaters? 'Mañana is soon enough.' Well, mañana better be right here and now!"

Jo weakly raised her head to object. "Cyn, it was just an accident. Really! I wasn't seriously injured!"

Cyn glared at her friend. "No thanks to this hotel! If you'd stepped into that empty shaft, you'd probably broken your leg or neck!" Cyn scowled at Octavia. "It's a miracle nothing happened!"

"I think," Octavia Dodd said quietly, "that Ms. Sharpe would like some quiet? Rest assured the matter will be throughly investigated."

Jo looked gratefully at the slender, dark-haired woman. Octavia appeared enchanting in a damask-rose dress and had probably been summoned from the party at the Piperade Restaurant below.

Cyn shot Jo an irritated glance as Jo leaned further back on the bed and nodded weakly in agreement. The two women departed, leaving the room bathed in cool moonlight. Jo closed her eyes, but couldn't shut out the images of falling.

The elevator shaft disappeared from her mind to be replaced by the luxurious New York apartment she and Glen had shared two years earlier. The telephone was shrilling and she had started down from the landing to the first floor, her hand trailing along the mahogany banister. In her mind, she saw the banister break and her body drop down heavily to the stairs; she was falling slowly, twisting downward, spiraling like an out-of-control top, crashing over one step at a time to the bottom.

The telephone had mercifully stopped the shrilling ring as she lay there, half-stunned, fearing for her unborn child. Then the pains had started, tearing through her body, knotting her up inside. Roland, their chauffeur, had heard her screaming and come inside to investigate. By the time Jo reached the hospital, the baby had aborted, born far too early to survive. Glen had been in Europe, negotiating a book contract for Ho-Jo Publications and had been delayed tracking down some author or other in the wilds of Scotland. So she had only the lime green walls of the barren hospital room, with its view of an outcropping back wall at the window, to keep her company.

The incident had completed the unraveling of her marriage. Once he was located, Glen had come as fast as his private Whisper-jet could bring him. His shocked appearance at the sight of his wife was only offset by the shock of losing his child. Jo was hurt and felt guilty about the fall, and found herself looking for a scapegoat in her husband, who had not been close at hand. The words which she had screamed in her agony at learning she could not have another baby couldn't be forgiven or forgotten by either of them.

Jo winced and opened her eyes. The suite with its white wicker furniture and parrot-colored bedspreads met her gaze. The inquisitive green monkey peered down at her from the picture over her bed. Gone was the New York apartment, where her baby had died.

Cyn was sleeping soundly in the other huge bed in the suite. Her friend had dumped clothes right and left in a steady line from the doorway to the closet to the bed. Jo tripped over her shoes as she navigated her way through the hallway and sitting room, and out onto the balcony.

The party had died down hours ago; the barbecue grill was just a pile of red charcoal in the enormous pit by the restaurant. Some of the guests were swimming out by the diving platform under a veiled moon with dark shadows across their faces. There was a stillness about the gardens below; the sweet fragrances wafted upward on the faint breeze which blew off of the water. The scent was suffocating, with a heaviness that reminded Jo of a woman wearing too much perfume.

Suddenly Jo had had enough of the beautiful island. Too many memories haunted her daylight hours. It was time to go home.

* * *

"Are you sure you're feeling well enough to leave today? I'm positive we could stay over for a few days. Hell, be generous! We could stay over for a week or two!" Cyn Savene wandered back and forth in their suite at the Palm Terrace, diamond bracelet glittering, wearing a new jade-green traveling outfit she'd purchased the day before.

Jo was sprawled out in the comfortable wicker chair in the suite's sitting room. She studied her friend's face. Cyn was certainly upset; her makeup was slightly smeared and her polished, red nails had been bitten back, a sure sign that all was not right.

"I'm fine, Cyn." There was a discreet tap on the door; moments later Michael was on his way down the stairs with Jo's luggage.

"I'll call you as soon as I get in to New York." Cyn planted a quick kiss on Jo's cheek. "For heaven's sake, be careful! I'm beginning to wonder if this is the Garden of Eden it's cracked up to be!"

Jo reflected on her friend's words as she followed Michael down the steps. Garden of Eden. But there had been a serpent in that garden, hadn't there? Jo reached the ground floor and peeked through the palm trees. The beach house had its deserted vacant look, the same as when she had arrived. Yet her attention returned to it again and again. Was the beach house where the serpent was living? Had the serpent come out of its hole and caused the elevator accident last night? And what was Dr. Smita Baid's real reason for being in Barbados? As an additional accomplice of someone? Or more? Jo didn't believe the conference story for a single moment. What was her real motive for being here?

Jo walked inside toward the main desk. The "Out of Order" sign was plainly visible on the elevator from the night before. She was met by a worried Octavia Dodd, who's gaze shifted nervously from the floor to Jo's face and back again.

"Are you sure you are all right? We have a good hospital here on the island. The doctors are excellent. Trained in London!"

"I'm fine, Octavia. I was just a little upset last night, that's all. I had a beautiful time."

"And you found what you were looking for?" Octavia shifted uneasily from one foot to another.

Somebody certainly put the fear of God into her, Jo thought silently. I didn't think Cyn had it in her. But then she thought of her friend's outburst the night before, the way her eyes had narrowed into an angry squint, her mouth spouting like a volcano going off.

"Yes, I found what I was looking for." Jo thought back to the information she had discovered about the Barbadian pirate, Stede Bonnet, and about the visit she'd had with Turtle and his mother. More importantly, she now had a lead on the poisonous machineel trees.

Octavia still seemed anxious, despite Jo's reassurances. She kept looking over her shoulder, as though half-expecting the big bad wolf from Little Red Riding Hood to come jumping out. Or perhaps I'm the nervous one, Jo thought to herself, as she shook hands and walked through the elegant lobby out toward the car park.

"Are you okey-dokey, Jo?" a high-pitched, childish voice piped up.

"Turtle!" The boy was standing under a high poinciana tree, wearing a different tattered T-shirt, this one with a Batman insignia on the front, plus a pair of cutoff jeans. The shirt was black and made the grotesque hump on the child's back less obvious, even though it was several sizes too small.

Jo dropped down to the child's height. "I'm just fine, Turtle. It was only an accident with the elevator. But tell me, how did you know about it?"

Turtle grinned. "Not voodoo drums, that for sure." He hesitated. "This a small island. Everybody talks. Turtle listens, that's how I find things out."

Jo wondered silently who the everybody was. Octavia or Michael? Someone who worked at the hotel?

She shrugged. It wasn't that important. Unless the one who had done the talking knew that the elevator incident hadn't been an accident at all.

"So you leave now, Jo? Fly to United States?"

"Yes, Turtle, I'm going home. I found what I was seeking. So it's time to say good-bye."

"But you will come back." The child dropped his voice. "My mother read your fortune in the crystal after you left yesterday. And she said you would be back. She asked me to tell you. She thought . . . she thought you did not get your money's worth. So it is not good-bye. It is 'until next time!' "

Would she be back? Jo honestly wasn't sure enough to say one way or another. But it wouldn't do to disappoint Turtle.

"Perhaps your mother is right, Turtle. Until next time."

Jo glanced up as Turtle scampered off. Michael was looking nervously at his watch. She hurried toward the car and clambered into the back seat.

Octavia was standing in the hotel breezeway. She was waving and it was obvious her earlier anxiety had vanished.

"Until the next time!"

Did these people know something she didn't? Jo wondered silently. Then she smiled and waved back.

What the heck, maybe there was something to this. "Until the next time!"

Ten hours later, Jo had convinced herself that there would be no "next time." Her flight was exhausting and there was a massive delay getting out of Miami. Her baggage, what little there was, got lost. Jo wearily picked up her car at the local airport in Raleigh and drove towards Nag's Head and home.

She pulled into the parking lot at the Learned Owls just as Tara Cataldo was closing up for the day. Her assistant was wearing slacks and a shocking pink teeshirt with the words *"Quand Meme"* on the front, which Jo translated loosely from the French to mean "In spite of All." Crawling out of her car and looking around, Jo drew a long breath.

"Jo! Marlowe and I missed you so! He's inside, bedded down for the night."

Jo followed as Tara eased back inside the Learned Owls.

The two women went down into the lounge section of the store. Marlowe gave an inquiring yowl and dropped into Jo's lap.

"So how was your trip? Is Barbados as gorgeous as the brochures said? And did you find any leads on Stede Bonnet and the poison trees?"

"Yes, to all of your questions." Jo breathlessly told her what she had discovered.

"So the poison trees really do exist." Tara chewed thoughtfully at her lower lip. The eyes behind the horned-rimmed glasses narrowed.

"They definitely exist in Barbados. The question is, are any of them in this area? And was Blackbeard's treasure actually buried under them, the way Cristabel's diary said."

"Speaking of diary, your fish expert from the aquarium, Norman Switec called a couple of times. He left messages. It seems he's very anxious to see that diary."

Jo scowled. "I know. I half-promised I'd show it to him. He's been very helpful," she hastened to add. "It's just that I'm not sure I want Cristabel's private thoughts exposed to him, or anyone for that matter. Why, he'd end up writing a book about it, treasure or no treasure!"

Tara laughed. "I can see Norman Switec's tombstone now. 'Here lies one whose name is writ in water.' " She grinned. " 'Writ in water.' Fish expert? Get it, Jo?"

"Yes, Tara. I get it."

"So what's your next step? Aside from meeting the delectable Norman for dinner."

Jo raised an inquiring brow.

"He mentioned it either the second or third time he called. Said it was going to be a surprise. Maybe he's going to have the waiter sing 'yo-ho-ho' during the meal!"

Jo succumbed to laughter. "Not likely. Norm takes his pirate lore seriously. You should have seen how upset he was when Watson Wise dressed up as the bearded legend. No, it can't be that kind of surprise. Must be something else."

"And you're going?"

Jo thought for a second of Glen. "I'm not sure. I . . . just . . . don't know."

"Oh but you should! Norm sounds like a lot of fun to me. He's not as serious as Quintin, but he seems just as trustworthy and reliable. After all, he's in charge of a large portion of the dive boat. He would hardly have that kind of responsibility if he wasn't."

"You like him, don't you Tara?"

"I do. I just wish I were a little older, more his age. He thinks of me as a college kid. But he was so nice to us when Quint took me diving on the *Queen Anne's Revenge*. Didn't talk down to me at all! I think he's a prince!"

Jo furrowed her brows. "The wisdom of the young. Okay, you've convinced me. But there is someone else I need to talk to first. He knows more about this area than any other living soul."

Tara's lips formed the word, "Who?"

"Possum Slocum. He was a degreed historian at Dartmouth University before he came down here and went into the bindery and bookstore business. And he never left it behind. Used to probe around every nook and cranny in the region. And since he's retired now and has sold me the store, he'll have even more time to snoop around."

"And you think this Possum person might know if there are any poison trees out on Ocracoke Island?"

"Or anyplace else in this part of the world. He's an expert and what I need right now."

Jo leaned back and fell silent. Tara studied her face from under lowered lids. "You didn't ask, but he did call. Wanted to be sure you were O.K. and hadn't gotten swallowed by a fish or something."

Jo didn't need to ask who. She knew Tara spoke of her husband, Glen. And it wasn't a fish he was worried about, it was a murderer.

Suddenly Jo felt strangely comforted. Of course, it could have been Tara's light-hearted chatter, but somehow Jo didn't think so.

All at once, the long flight home caught up with her. As Jo barely suppressed a yawn, Tara caught a glimpse of it.

"I'd better go. You look half-dead on your feet." She withdrew her legs, which had been dangling over the blue armchair, and pulled herself upright. But instead of her characteristic amble out the door, she shifted almost nervously from one foot to another and back again.

Jo twitched open an eye. "You had something else to report, ensign?" she queried like a mock-drill sergeant.

"Actually, you'll think I'm crazy. It's just that . . . when I've opened up the store the last couple of days, I've had the feeling someone else had been inside. Watching or looking. Like . . . the vibrations in the force were disturbed or something. You know what I mean, maybe?"

"You sound like Obi-Wan Kenobi." Jo thought back. How many times when she was in Barbados had she felt someone was watching her? Just like what Tara was describing?

"I know what you mean. Maybe."

"Just be careful, Jo. People do nasty things when a lot of money is involved."

Glen had said almost the same thing to her once. She had thought he was exaggerating when he described the wars between the have and the have-nots in the world, and how underhanded and ugly they could become. Of course, she had considered Glen as a murder suspect, so perhaps he hadn't been so far wrong.

Tara continued nonstop, as was her fashion. "And if Blackbeard had a treasure and if he buried it and if it could be found . . ."

"Someone could get hurt if that someone were to get in the way. Roger, wilco, and out. I have received and digested your message. And I appreciate the thought."

"Just be careful when you see this Possum person. If he knows or has information worth a lot of money . . ."

"He could be in danger, too." Jo's eyes flickered open. She watched Tara give Marlowe a final pat and saunter out the door. Moments later, the little car Tara drove gave a cough as the engine started and her assistant pulled out into the road.

Jo rose and wandered back into her office, trailed by Marlowe. The cat hopped up onto the bookcase and settled down between a copy of Hemingway's *The Sun Also Rises* and Margaret Mitchell's *Gone with the Wind.*

Was Marlowe trying to say something? He had chosen to lay between volumes which portrayed strong women who knew what they wanted and went out to get it. Lady Brett Ashley and Scarlett O'Hara had both been thwarted in the true love department, mainly by their single-mindedness and ambition.

Jo thought back to the time right after she had fallen down the stairs and lost her baby. Her marriage to Glen had begun unraveling like the string on a beach kite that had flown too high on the wind. She and her husband had made a lunch date to try and make up at the Plaza Hotel; he had brought her a copy of *The Sun Also Rises,* autographed by its well-known author. But their lunch had deteriorated to a name-calling contest with Glen comparing her to Lady Brett Ashley, who married for money rather than love, and who left Jake high and dry in the last chapter, symbolizing the superficial atmosphere in which they both lived.

Although her response, "You've read *The Sun Also Rises* too? Gee, so literate? I thought you never got beyond magazines, and trashy ones at that," was hardly intended to appease or make up. Jo had stormed from the restaurant in a fury, determined to perform all future communication through her attorney.

The divorce papers lay on the desk, still neither sent nor signed. Jo studied them for a long moment. She had been so sure that the divorce was what she wanted.

Jo closed her eyes. For some reason the crazy song "Come Josephine in your Flying Machine" ran through her mind. Perhaps it was because she was undecided or possibly it was because Glen had teased her about it at their first meeting and called her Josephine ever since.

Jo paused, her pen poised over the divorce papers. Then

she slowly folded the documents up and placed them back in the envelope. She was just fooling herself. She wasn't sure that a divorce was what she wanted. Not anymore. And not in the slightest.

Chapter Fourteen

Because I could not stop for Death,
He kindly stopped for me—
The Carriage held but just Ourselves
And Immortality.
                                        —Emily Dickinson

"**C**mon over!" Possum Slocum boomed over the phone to Jo the next morning when she called him right after breakfast. Jo was standing in her apartment above the bookstore, looking out on the azure blue of the ocean, with its wispy bits of wave cascading up onto the beach. The sky was a gilly-flower blue with the birds circling like gray phantoms overhead, emitting strident squawks of seeming glee whenever one pulled a fish from the sea. It was early, but already hot; beachgoers were sprawled under umbrellas, while children and the occasional dog frisked to and fro.

"I've been anxious to talk to you and find out how the bookstore is doing," Possum added as an afterthought. "I'm painting now. Sell the things in an art shop in Manteo not far from Festival Park. Roanoke Island is overrun with tourists, but I don't complain. They buy my artwork and keep the island's economy up."

"I have this diary, Possum." Jo explained about the record of Cristabel Lamonte's life. "I'd like you to take a look. She talks about Blackbeard's treasure and poison trees."

"Trees, you say? And treasure, too? That does it. Now you've got my curiosity itched up. I'm over on Roanoke. Right off of Route 64 on Herriott Road."

"Herriott like James, who wrote *All Creatures Great and Small?*"

Possum cackled. "You got it. Andy Griffith lives right around the corner from me and down the road apiece. Although everybody is kind of right around the corner, since I'm sort of in the middle of the island. But good old Andy, he likes to keep a low profile."

Jo had been scribbling directions. "I don't suppose Opie is hiding over there somewhere too?"

Possum emitted another loud chuckle. "Naw. No Opie. You just come over on the Manteo Causeway and hang a right through the middle of town. If you get to the Elizabethan Gardens, you've gone too far. And," he paused for a second, "you can meet Bobbi while you're here!"

"Bobbi?"

"My significant other. She lives in half of my duplex. She'd like to meet you. Loves books almost as much as I do, and knows a lot about antiques too."

"Possum! You have a girlfriend!"

Jo could almost see the old man grinning over the phone.

"At my age too. Heck, Jo, if there's hope for me, there's hope for anyone! I'll tell Bobbi to put the kettle on. She makes Tarheel hush puppies that will curl your toes!"

Jo laughed. "I'm hooked, Possum! I'll be over shortly. Tea and hush puppies. How can I say no?"

Possum was cackling as Jo hung up the telephone. She pulled the leather bound diary from its hiding place behind Betty Crocker.

"I'm glad that cookbook Possum left me finally came in handy. I sure never learned to cook from it!" Jo said aloud to Marlowe. The cat was sprawled on the window seat, studying two gray gulls intently through the glass. The gray gulls were eyeing him rather nervously back.

Jo jammed the diary into her purse and hesitated. Then she dialed Norman Switec's number.

"Jo! You're back! And how was Barbados? No, don't

tell me now. Have dinner with me! I have a Blackbeard surprise for you and we can catch up on everything that's been going on."

Jo felt her spirits lighten still more as she arranged to meet Norm that evening.

"Well, Marlowe, I'll be seeing you later."

Jo grasped her purse and a wide-brimmed straw hat to keep out the sun. She crossed through the arched doorway to the outside staircase, after leaving a note for Tara hitched over the cash register. Jo climbed into her Chevy and headed for the Nag's Head Causeway and across the bay to Roanoke Island.

She followed Old Nag's Head Road past the triangular-shaped Whalebone Junction, then over the causeway and through Manteo. The causeway was relatively empty of traffic; there were as many bicycle riders out on the road as cars. The cycles dipped and swooped almost like the gulls out on Shallowbag Bay.

Turning left onto Herriott Road, Jo spotted Possum's century-old white Victorian farmhouse surrounded by live oaks. A small creek, which led to Croatan Sound, meandered along on the edge of the property. Crabpots were stacked up, giving her a good idea of what Possum did when he wasn't painting. Two rocking chairs with a step-stool adorned the veranda, while a second door and staircase, obviously the duplex where Possum's friend lived, led toward the second floor. Carolina wrens were busy constructing a nest under the eves of the porch, and Jo heard several mockingbirds and kingfishers calling to each other as she parked the car and ambled toward the front door.

Possum had a lovely vegetable garden trimmed with the conch shells so common in the area. As Jo followed the sandy path up the front steps, the screen door opened and Possum Slocum stuck a bearded head out.

"Jo! Glad you made it!" Possum boomed out. He held out a work-worn hand to her in greeting, his grin wide with spontaneous laughter that crinkled up the blue eyes behind the dark-lensed glasses. Possum had been working at his trade; he wore a paint-splattered blue T-shirt and jeans, plus tennis shoes typical of Roanoke islanders. The tattoo on his right arm, from his early days in the Navy, was of a smiling mermaid, whose tail danced as Possum flexed his arm.

He led Jo inside and offered her the traditional lemonade of the Carolinas. Jo shoved off her wide-brimmed hat and glanced around the room; the furniture was worn, the couch lumpy, yet she felt the radiating warmth of home. A bookcase sat in one corner, with contents pulled every which way, while Possum's easel and paints stood by the window to catch the outside light.

Possum trotted back from a second room, logically the kitchen, with Jo's drink and a German beer for himself. He eased down into the cushioned rocker, which creaked under his weight.

"I haven't exactly lost any weight since I retired. Bobbi cooks too good, that's the problem. Every time I try to lose a few pounds, she bakes up one of her special upside-down cakes or talks me into going down to the Wilted Raddish for a German dinner and beer."

"You look great, Possum. And you mentioned Bobbi on the phone. She must be taking good care of you!"

"Uh-huh. She rents the upstairs place, but she's out shopping right now. I think Bobbi thought you might want to see me alone, what with a mysterious diary and all."

Jo fished Cristabel's book out of her voluminous straw handbag. "I'm not sure how mysterious it is. Mainly just a girl's life back in the early 1700's. Until she was kidnapped by Blackbeard, of course."

Possum took the leather-bound volume and lovingly smoothed it open. "The dates are right, that's one thing. This seems to have happened about six months before Blackbeard was defeated in battle and killed off Ocracoke. Lieutenant Maynard cut off his head and left it dangling from the mast of the ship."

He flipped slowly through the pages and sniffed the paper. "They don't make books like this anymore. Now it's all factory glue, cardboard, and Book-of-the-Month Club binding."

"I know. The part about the trees is toward the end. She

escaped off the *Queen Anne's Revenge* with the help of the cabin boy and swam to shore. That's where she talks about the poison trees down close to the water. When burned, the trees blistered her hands and made her eyes sting. The pirates buried the treasure chests and returned to the ship. Cristabel ran off in the opposite direction and eventually met up with the cabin boy. That's when the diary ends. But there's no clue about exactly where they were, except for the business about the poison trees."

"The trees," Jo added informationally, "could be the machineel. But I've never heard of any on Ocracoke. Or on Cedar Island, either."

Possum closed his eyes for a moment. "Machineel trees," he mused. "Now where have I heard that name before?"

Jo looked hopeful.

The old man rattled on. "My father, I think. He said they reminded him of the mustard gas during the war. World War I, that is. He was stationed in Europe and the Central Powers used it against us. The gas caused sneezing and coughing, with skin blistering like from the sun. Eyes would start to burn like fire and eyelids would swell up. The nervous system would be affected if exposure was for a long enough time. My father said those trees were kind of like the gas. That was why they got rid of the lot, because they didn't want the tourists accidently coming in contact with them. But it wasn't on Ocracoke Island." Possum shook his head slowly. "I just can't recall. My memory isn't what it used to be and my father has been dead these thirty-five years."

The older man sipped his beer. "Let me think on it. Could you leave the diary and call me tomorrow morning? If I'm going to do any recollecting, hopefully I'll remember by then. It's in those books," he waved a negligent hand at the overloaded bookcase, "somewhere. I'll just have to tinker around and dig it out."

"No computers for you, then, Possum?" Jo asked as she handed him the diary.

"No!" the old man almost spat back. "Computers are the work of the devil! Worst blight on modern society.

Anything that can be completely disabled by pulling a plug—"

The door opened and shut from the outside veranda, interrupting him mid-sentence. Footsteps came toward the main room, hesitated, and stopped.

"Bobbi? Is that you? Come on in and see who's here. Jo Sharpe, the lady who bought my old bookstore!"

A woman's head poked around the corner. She was wearing dark glasses and a scarf pulled low over her face. As she entered the room, she smiled down lovingly at Possum and then held out a hand to Jo.

"I'm so pleased to meet you at last."

Jo racked her memory. "I know you," she murmured aloud, shaking hands. Then her eyes widened as recollection came. "You are that actress! Bobbi Partridge! Of course I should have known the name! You play Queen Elizabeth at the playhouse in town, that one-woman show. And over at the Lost Colony Theatre." Jo turned to Possum. "Why didn't you tell me who your friend was?" she exclaimed almost accusingly.

"Because I like to live a normal life, if possible." Bobbi smiled and went to perch on the corner of Possum's chair. She removed the scarf and glasses. "Believe it or not, theatre people would rather just be treated like anyone else."

"I've enjoyed your performances. And I'm glad I finally got to tell you so!"

Bobbi lovingly smoothed back Possum's thin white hair, which was sticking out over one ear. "I trust you two had a nice chat." Bobbi was thin, almost gangly—all arms, elbows, and legs, which the forest green pants suit she wore could not disguise. She reached gracefully over to take a sip of Possum's beer. Bobbi wasn't beautiful; her hair was rather lanky and her skin seemed dry, probably from the heavy makeup she wore on stage. But her expression when she looked at the older man was so full of love that her appearance was not important. Jo thought she was perhaps half of Possum's age, but that seemed unimportant too.

Jo watched the two of them together. They were lovers, there was no question in her mind. Something happened when Possum looked at Bobbi and she looked back, something beautiful that only occurs when two people care about each other very, very much.

Jo thought back. Had she and Glen ever looked at each other like that? Like they were the only two people in the world? Perhaps in the beginning, before all of the dark, nasty things had happened. Perhaps their love had been pure and unadulterated a long, long time ago.

Jo tore her eyes away. She felt a stab of jealousy and a stab of sorrow go through her, although she wasn't sure exactly why. She finished the lemonade in one gulp and stood up to leave.

"I'll call you tomorrow, Possum. Maybe something will turn up in all that." She looked in the direction of the bookcase. "But if not, I'd still like to talk again."

"Right, Jo." Possum pulled his gaze from Bobbi. "I'll check for you. I'm sure there was something and perhaps it will come back to me."

Bobbi moved as if to rise, but Jo waved her back with a smile. "I can find the way. And . . . I can certainly see why retirement is agreeing with Possum. You take care now."

As Jo opened and shut the front door, the other two were still staring at each other. She doubted that they even heard her leave.

Tara Cataldo was ensconced in her favorite place behind the cash register at the door of the Learned Owls, wobbling back and forth on a chair, when Jo returned. Her young assistant was reading the ending of Stevenson's *Treasure Island*, while keeping a careful eye on three children who were sprawled on plastic furniture in the children's area and watching the video of Disney's *Cinderella*. Their mother was rummaging through the travel books on North Carolina, which were arranged haphazardly on shelves toward the back of the store.

Tara sighed and looked up from her book as Jo dumped her purse down on a chair and collapsed next to Marlowe on a sofa.

"Boy, treasure hunting was never easy, even back in the days of Robert Louis Stevenson," Tara mumbled, bending back the top corner of a page as a place holder. "I should have stuck with the video of this book. I think I would have been happier."

Jo lay on the sofa and let the waves of air conditioning in the store wash over her. "Which video version?" she cocked an eyebrow at Tara and said tongue-in-cheek, "There were three. Which one has the happy ending?"

"Why Disney's, of course!" Tara didn't realize Jo spoke in jest. "Disney never has bad endings. Nobody dies, nobody even gets hurt. At least not so they can't recover."

Jo smiled. "Too bad it's not like that in real life."

"Yeah." Tara came out from behind the desk. Today her T-shirt was white with lime green stripes and a purple heart right in the middle; her outfit was topped off with the usual jeans and sandals. She flopped down across from Jo in one of the lounge chairs.

"By the way, I think our coffeemaker died. Again. It kind of gurgled, but nothing came out when I first got here. Considering the heat, it's not that important." She looked at Jo quizzically. "So give. What did Possum Slocum say about the diary?"

"Actually, I have to call back tomorrow. He wasn't sure. He thinks he might remember something his father told him years ago. Maybe! So I left the diary with him to study. Possum is one of the few people I trust completely." And Glen, too, Jo thought to herself. At least she had before the divorce. Maybe part of her was beginning to again.

"I don't think those machi...mach...poison trees could be around here now. Too many tourists. Can you see the headlines, 'Tourist Poisoned by Local Tree?' " She shook her head. "No way. Those trees likely met the chopping block years ago. It's bad enough when the visitors end up with heatstroke over at the Outer Banks Hospital. And that isn't really anybody's fault but their own!"

"Very true." Jo thought of all the warnings she'd seen in the local newspaper about problems with the heat. "People do seem to make their own trouble sometimes."

Tara gave her a long, slant-eyed look. "Quite right." She readjusted her position in the chair. "I meant to tell you. The delectable fish expert from the aquarium called. He wanted to talk to you, but I told him you had gone to see Possum to ask him about the diary. Norm said he was stuck in traffic and was going to have to cancel dinner." Tara pushed her owl-rimmed glasses back up in the general direction of her nose. "I guess we will have to wait to find out about his Blackbeard surprise."

Jo eased to her feet. "What a shame. I'll ring him back. But first I'd better get up to the office and take care of a few bills."

Suddenly the three children at the video monitor began shrieking excitedly about something which had happened to Cinderella on the screen. Jo glanced their way before she continued. "And I want to call Cyn in New York, too. Hopefully she should be back by now."

"Unless she missed the plane again. Oops, here comes my customer."

Jo looked up as a haggard woman with dark circles under her eyes moved to the cash register. As Tara rang up her purchase, she asked hesitantly, "Would it be okay if the kids stayed 'til the end of the movie? I don't think I could pry them away right now."

Tara grinned. "I don't think you could either. Take all the time you want. I'll even make you a cup of tea!"

Jo stepped back as the two women relaxed in the lounge area. Tara was a loyal, true-blue employee and friend. Jo suddenly felt lucky to have her.

The phone shrilled, waking Jo at 1:00 the following morning. She leaned over Marlowe, who was lying on her bed and glared at the instrument like it was a carrier of death.

"Hello," Jo mumbled, her eyes feeling like she'd only been asleep for five minutes.

It was her assistant, Tara.

"Jo, did you see? It was just on the news. Possum Slocum has been murdered. His throat was cut with a knife. And . . ." here Tara paused to catch her breath, "the chief of police told the reporters that Glen Howard has been taken in for questioning!"

Chapter Fifteen

'Oh no, no,' said the little Fly, 'for I've often
heard it said,
They never, never wake again who sleep upon
your bed!'
     —Mary Howitt, *The Spider and the Fly*

"I just don't see how your going over there now is going
to help Glen," Tara Cataldo said to Jo the following morning. The two were in the lounge area of the Learned Owls.
Tara had arrived a little before 9:00, decked out in a puce-
colored T-shirt with cutoff jeans and black-beaded moc-
casins.

"I mean, for months now you've been saying you want
a divorce, and now . . ." She studied Jo thoughtfully.

"I know! It doesn't make much sense to me, either. But
look there . . ." Jo had flicked the remote on the small television set that she used to entertain the children while their
parents hunted for books in the store. The 9:00 morning
news with Hugh Montgomery was just coming on. The
newscaster was talking live from right outside the courthouse in Manteo. The familiar street with the centuries-old
building surrounded by a grove of ancient oak trees
appeared. Jo narrowed her eyes, watching intently as the
camera swooped in on Glen and his attorney, Sarah James,
an attractive forty-year-old brunette wearing a dark blue

business suit with a red scarf wound around her slender throat. Glasses completed the picture.

Jo heard Sara James mutter "No comment!" to the innumerable questions posed by the reporters, as Glen eased off of the courthouse veranda and into a waiting limo. The car whisked the two of them down the drive, leaving the press frantically snapping pictures.

"And for those of you just joining us, that was multimillionaire Glen Howard, head of the conglomerate of Ho-Jo Publications, and Sarah James, his attorney, who has just flown in to Manteo by private jet from New York. Mr. Howard was taken in for questioning in the recent murder of a local resident, Peter Slocum, also known as 'Possum.' Slocum specialized in painting scenery of the Carolina Capes." The announcer's voice continued on, giving pertinent details of Possum's life, including his service in the Second World War.

Then the cameras swooped in again, live, for an interview with the detective handling the murder investigation, Jack Wolfe.

"Isn't that the same cop who was investigating Watson Wise's accident on the *Queen Anne's Revenge?*" Tara hissed an aside to Jo.

"Yes! It certainly is! But hush! Maybe we can find out why they took Glen in for questioning!"

Strangely enough, Jo minded that the police thought Glen had committed the crime. They should know how I felt after getting stuck on the *Queen Anne's Revenge* for the night, she thought ironically. But that was different. She had felt trapped, humiliated, and very angry.

The camera zoomed in for a close-up of Wolfe.

"And have you any evidence directly linking Mr. Howard with Possum Slocum?" a reporter was asking.

Wolfe cleared his throat. "Yes, we do, but I'm not at liberty to say exactly what it is.

"I wonder what they found?" Tara asked aloud.

"Shush!" Jo hissed as Wolfe continued.

"Rest assured we plan to do everything possible to bring the murderer to justice."

"Have you any other suspects besides Glen Howard, then?"

Jack Wolfe wet his lips nervously. "We're working on it," he finally muttered aloud.

Jo flicked off the television and wearily pressed her hands to her temples.

"We're working on it? Can't that guy come up with a different tune?"

The telephone shrilled suddenly, sounding overly loud in the quiet bookstore. Marlowe had been napping alongside of Jo; he raised an inquisitive head, his large eyes crossed, and stared at the two women.

Tara picked up the telephone as Jo turned back to the television. The camera crew had focused on Possum Slocum's home with its long veranda and rocking chair on the front porch—which would be permanently empty from now on—and his vegetable garden, whose crop would not be eaten. Jo wondered for a moment where Bobbi Partridge was. Perhaps she had collapsed from the shock of learning of Possum's murder. Reporters were swarming around the empty house. Jo reflected that Possum would say they resembled fleas going after a hound dog. Sadly she wondered if the old man had died instantly, and if he knew who had killed him.

Tara's voice droned on in the background before she hung up and turned back to Jo.

"You were talking about wanting to see Glen. I know where he can be found," she stated succinctly.

Jo was nonplussed. "But how? Everybody on Roanoke Island wants to know where Mr. Howard can be found. Those reporters want nothing better than to run him into ground. Where can he have gone to hide? He can't leave the area because of his bond."

Tara had a cat-who-swallowed-the-canary expression. "That," she indicated the phone, "was Quint."

"The *Queen Anne's Revenge* Quint? Why did he call?"

"To tell us that the dive boat, which is also a glorified cruise ship, if you remember, was ordered from the dive site in Beaufort and told to drop anchor off the island of

Roanoke late last night. And guess who has just come on board to escape the rapacious reporters and talk to his attorney?"

Tara answered her own question. "The head of Ho-Jo Publications and chief financial backer of Scisearch, who is sponsoring the expedition."

"So Glen is on board!" Jo breathed out slowly.

"And Quint is willing to ferry you out there in the skiff. I implied that you had some information that might help Mr. Howard. Be sure and come up with something. Quint seems to be a fan of your husband and rather taken with him. So whenever you are ready, you need only drive over to the Elizabethan Gardens and call Quint on your cell phone. I've got the number. And be careful you're not followed, especially by reporters." Tara leaned back, a satisfied expression on her face. Jo looked flabbergasted and for once, wordless.

"And that," the younger woman said archly, "is a good piece of detective work, if I do say so myself!"

"Yo, Jo!" Glad you made it!" Quint's voice came out loud and clear over the cell phone.

Jo had followed his instructions. She left her car in the parking lot at the Elizabethan Gardens at the north end of Roanoke Island, and was waiting patiently down by the shore line for the young man to appear with the surfboat.

"I'm on my way. Hang in there."

Quint hung up, and a few moments later Jo heard the sound of the surfboat approaching shore. She ran down toward the water, past the wild sea-oats and the fire-colored gaillardia dotting the beach. Albemarle Sound was a serpentine color, with milky wavelets washing up onto the sand. Jo splashed through the shallow water as Quint pulled closer to shore. He waved and helped her climb aboard before turning the boat around and heading north.

Moments later Quint skillfully drew the surfboat alongside the dive boat, which seemed to be looking more like a cruise ship all the time. He helped Jo crawl over the gunwale onto the main deck, before securing the smaller boat.

She glanced behind her at the sky. It was going to rain and sometime soon. Early summer wasn't the storm season but there were always orphan, tropical depressions—the stray clouds which carried a deluge to the islands.

She turned back as Quint began talking. "He's not expecting you," the young man spoke over his shoulder. "He and that attorney from New York have been closeted on the upper deck. But they both look worried. That's why when Tara told me you had spoken to Possum just hours before he died, well, I thought you could help."

Quint turned back, his young face wracked by indecision. "I wasn't supposed to let anyone out here. But," he added ingeniously, "you're not just anybody. You are still officially Mrs. Howard!"

"You did the right thing, Quint. I'm going to try and help untangle this mess. But I need to talk to Glen and find out exactly what this evidence is that links him to Possum. It must be something pretty damning. Detective Wolfe didn't impress me as the sort of man to rush around asking idle questions, or making unfounded arrests. At least, he didn't after Watson Wise died."

"You're right. That detective seemed to me to be half-asleep. Well, he's wide awake now. But I don't know what this mysterious evidence is. Maybe Mr. Howard can tell you."

"I'll find my way to his suite. I remember the layout of the ship." Jo left Quint energetically tying up the surfboat and looking much happier.

She pulled open the nearest door on the main deck. The ship's layout wasn't that complicated; the Romanov Salon met her gaze with its garish red and black decor, reminiscent of Czar Peter I and Catherine, two of the unhappy Romanovs. Money did not bring them happiness, that was for sure. Jo shrugged and put past history out of her mind; there were enough problems in the present to deal with.

She peered into the high room; the salon was empty. Jo thought back to the first time she had been on board and the elegant dinner Glen had hosted. Everyone had been alive and well then, before Watson had gotten drunk and fallen over the side. *Fallen,* her intuitive self questioned, *or pushed?* Suddenly Jo wasn't sure. At the time the snail expert's death had seemed an unfortunate accident, but after Possum's murder, it seemed it could have been very deliberate. Watson had been a short, stocky man; even without the liquor, it wouldn't have been so very hard for someone to bash him over the head and then push him into the sound. Even for a woman. Jo wondered if Detective Wolfe had considered that the killer could be female. There had been enough women on board that night: herself, Smita Baid, Janna Lawrence, plus Janna's staff from Ho-Jo Publications that she couldn't seem to travel without. The question remained as to why. Why would anyone want to kill Watson Wise, a snail expert, of all things? Drugs, as Tara had implied? Blackmail? Unless the killer were crazy. Jo shuddered. Suddenly she didn't like where her thoughts were leading. Suppose Glen had caved in under the pressure. Pressure of running a world-wide publishing empire, pressure from her over the divorce, pressure and unhappiness from losing their first child?

Jo half-ran past the Romanov Salon to the stairs at the end of the companionway. There was an elevator, but after what had happened at the Palm Terrace in Barbados, she decided the exercise would be good for her.

Reaching the upper deck, Jo paused to catch her breath. Here was the suite where she had stayed so briefly, along with the captain's quarters and Glen Howard's rooms, when he chose to stay on board. The colors were far more muted and Jo suspected Glen had gotten a decorator on the dive boat to tone down the garish effect still visible in the main salon.

She padded down the companionway with its rich charcoal-gray carpeting and fake Impressionist paintings on the wall. Although maybe they weren't fake paintings. Maybe they were the real thing. Sometimes it was so hard to tell the real from the imitation, Jo thought idly to herself. Artwork, designer dresses, love? Who could say what was sometimes real and sometimes fake? Even experts had trouble. And Jo knew she was no expert.

She rapped sharply on the door of the gigantic suite at the end of the companionway and waited. Long seconds ticked by. Then the door was yanked open, and a voice Jo scarcely recognized snarled out, "I thought I made it plain I didn't want to be disturbed! I thought . . ." Then the dark-haired business tycoon, who had enough money to topple governments in foreign countries, really looked at who was standing there.

"Hello, Glen. I was in the neighborhood and I thought I'd drop in."

Glen Howard ran a hand over his face and rubbed his red-rimmed eyes. "What in the hell are you doing here?" he asked shortly.

Before he had time to slam the door, Jo edged past and into his room.

Chapter Sixteen

There would have been a time for such a word,
Tomorrow, and tomorrow, and tomorrow.
—Shakespeare, *Macbeth*

"Come in, why don't you. You couldn't get out of here fast enough the last time you were on board." Glen shoved the door shut with a crash that half-knocked it off its hinges. He turned, his eyes watching Jo. "What are you out here for anyway? Did you come to gloat?"

"I came to help because I don't think you killed Possum. I don't think you could kill anyone." Having said what she'd thought for a long time, Jo took a good look at Glen. She had never seen him quite like this, not even when their daughter had died. There was no hint of the usual well-tailored appearance that reeked of good taste; Glen's shirt and slacks were wrinkled and looked like he had slept in them. There was a faint stubble of beard, and his eyes held a strange expression. It was like he was looking down a tunnel and couldn't see the end. Jo remembered something her mother had said years before: "Wealthy people don't get that way by playing by the rules. They are cold, ruthless, and self-seeking. Not inherited money. That's different. I'm talking about the pull-themselves-up-by-their-bootstraps kind."

Her mother should know, Jo thought defensively. But

141

Glen? Was Glen cut from the same cloth, so to speak? And was the murder of a harmless old man an event woven into that cloth? Suddenly Jo shivered, although the room was not cold.

A woman was approaching the small gladiator's circle where Jo and Glen were squaring off. She reeked of money in a well-tailored business suit and alligator pumps and purse, which Jo suspected were the real thing. She held out a manicured hand with pearl gray fingernail polish and a Bucherer watch on her wrist with twenty different ways to tell time.

"How do you do? My name is Sarah James, Mr. Howard's attorney. And you are . . ."

Jo and Glen spoke at the same time. Her "Josephine Howard" was drowned out by his acid-toned "Ms. Josephine Sharpe." Sarah James raised her brows in silent inquiry. She even has well-manicured brows, Jo thought savagely to herself.

The other woman sized up the situation between the two combatants with a practiced eye. Jo wondered if she had been a divorce lawyer in an earlier life, as Sarah James waltzed her over to the soft, mohair sofa in the sitting room and went to fetch coffee from a sterling coffee set.

Jo stole a look around, but aside from Glen and his attorney, the place seemed empty.

As though reading her thoughts, Glen correctly interpreted her glance. "Don't worry, Jo. Nobody else is here, aside from Sarah and myself. And you're free to make of that what you will."

Jo thought back to the words she and Glen had spoken to each other when their daughter had died and bit her tongue. They would get nowhere if they began throwing accusations back and forth, which had always been the pattern to their discussions after she'd had her accident. And they'd gotten nowhere that way.

Sarah James swished back over the plush, battleship-gray carpeting with Jo's coffee. Jo could smell the rich, expensive scent of Joy perfume on the other woman's wrists as she handed over the cup. Suddenly Jo thought her own Blue Grass scent smelled tacky.

Sarah James assumed correctly that she'd better take control of the conversation from the start, if anything were to be gained at this meeting.

"Now, Jo, you made an enormous effort to find Glen and get yourself out here." She sipped her own coffee. "Would you mind telling me why?"

Glen snorted. He moved over to the fireplace mantle, pulled a cigarette from an ebony box, and lit it. "Isn't it plain, Sarah? Josephine isn't happy unless she's sticking her little, pointed nose in somebody else's business. In this case, mine." He glowered at both women equally.

Sarah's eyes reflected surprise and something else. Her expression turned thoughtful and enigmatic as she waited patiently for Jo to answer.

Jo gulped her coffee. It was too hot and burned her tongue, but she couldn't have cared less. Glen was puffing away on his cigarette, lounging almost casually in the large armchair by the fireplace. It occurred to Jo that he had started smoking again somewhere along the line since she'd left him. Well, maybe the man had a good reason.

"I heard about what had happened on the television, early this morning," Jo began. "And I'd seen Possum Slocum the day before he died. I was supposed to call him back tomorrow, I mean today. And I thought that perhaps I might have heard or seen something that would help Glen's case."

Sarah James' eyes reflected her interest. "What did you and Possum discuss, if you don't mind my asking?"

"Not at all. I'd come into possession of a diary written three hundred years ago by Cristabel Lamonte. She had some information about Blackbeard and his buried treasure." Jo continued and told the attorney the story of the poison trees and the young, black slave who had helped Cristabel escape from Blackbeard's *Queen Anne's Revenge.*

Sarah James knit her brows thoughtfully. "This whole case seems to come back to Blackbeard and that accursed ship." At Jo's glance of surprise, she continued. "What linked Glen to Possum Slocum was his watch. A Rolex.

The police found it under the old man's body, almost as though the victim had grappled with his assailant before the murderer cut his throat with a knife."

"A Rolex?"

"The Rolex. The one you gave me on our first anniversary inscribed with my name," Glen interrupted harshly. "The thing had gone missing the night Watson Wise died down on the dive boat. He'd been dancing around drunk, doing that ridiculous imitation of Blackbeard. Anyway, I'd helped him over to a chair. He was drunk as a skunk, but he was my guest. I guess I felt responsible. Then I saw you leave along with Norman Switec and Smita Baid. You remember, we met as you were going on deck. And somewhere along the line, the watch vanished."

"Did you go back and look?" Jo queried softly.

"Of course. I had the captain, Edward Hornos, tear the salon apart. But no watch," Glen stated bluntly. "I'll be honest and say I thought Watson Wise could have lifted it when I was helping him. It was a valuable watch, Josephine. As you should know. Nobody else was really close enough to me. But if that were so, and Watson had jammed it in his pocket to hawk later at some pawnshop, it should have gone over the side with him. And it didn't. It turned up under Possum Slocum. A man I'd never met in my life!"

Glen's expression was one of bewilderment. He'd always prided himself on keeping abreast of every situation and controlling it at the same time. Here was something he couldn't begin to explain, much less control.

"Is that all they have? Just the watch?" Jo looked at Sarah, but she was really asking the question of Glen.

"Isn't that enough?"

Sarah James shot him an annoyed glance. "Unfortunately, Glen doesn't have an alibi for either of the two deaths. He was alone when Watson Wise went over the side, and again last night when Possum was murdered." She shrugged. "The police can't prove he was there, except for the watch. He can't prove he wasn't."

"It could have been planted by someone," Jo muttered under her breath.

Glen scowled. "Yeah, but unfortunately the guy who would have done the planting was already dead."

"There was something else. One of Possum's neighbors said she thought she saw a man walking down Herriott Road to the house. But she didn't get a particularly good look. It was dark and she wasn't even sure it was a man."

Jo looked silently at Sarah James.

"Under police questioning, she admitted that it could have been a woman. She just wasn't sure. But you can see why the police jumped the way they did. If Glen had had an alibi things would be different, but there was nothing."

"Yeah." Glen Howard stubbed out his cigarette savagely in a crystal-cut ashtray. "I was tired and I went home to bed. Alone. The police seemed to find that idea as preposterous as the rest of my story."

"But it's all circumstantial," Jo said slowly. "And there must be some other explanation."

"If you think you're getting any information out of Detective Wolfe, you're wasting your time," Sarah James said shortly. "He wasn't just tight with the facts, he was silent as the proverbial grave."

"But Wolfe didn't strike me as being stupid. Just the opposite. Just suppose," and Jo hesitated before her words started tumbling out, "suppose Wolfe doesn't have the time or manpower to investigate every last aspect of the case. And he figures that by arresting Glen, the wealthy Mr. Howard will launch his own investigation. He does have the time, money, and a high-priority motive to catch the real murderer. So Glen hires you, Ms. James, and starts looking into things himself." Jo stopped. "What do you think? Is it a possibility?" She asked Sarah James the question, but she was looking at Glen Howard for the answer.

"Not bad, Josephine. Not bad at all." There was something beyond mere appreciation in her husband's eyes. Something quite unreadable, that Jo couldn't quite fathom.

"Unless," and here Sarah James cut in, her voice as cool as moonstone, "they really believe he is guilty, and that he killed Possum Slocum!"

* * *

A couple of hours later, the three had dived and zigzaged over and around the facts an endless number of times. No solution was in sight. Jo sighed and rubbed her eyes. Glen had returned to the fireplace to light another cigarette. Sarah James flexed a hand and capped the pen she had been making notations with for hours.

"We'll keep in touch," Sarah murmured softly. "And I'll call personally if I hear anything more. Right now I need to start assimilating all of this information."

Jo nodded and moved to collect her shoes, which had somehow gotten shoved under one of the high-backed chairs. She slipped them on, picked up her keys, and edged toward the door of the suite.

Glen pushed himself away from the desk where he had been lounging, and followed.

Jo opened the door and ambled down the companionway, Glen at her heels. She turned at the stairs.

"I know. There's an elevator. But after the incident in Barbados . . ."

"You'd rather take the stairs. Not surprising." Glen paused, his eyes studying her face. "When you first came in, I got the distinct impression that you were expecting to see someone. Someone other than Sarah and myself, that is."

Jo shrugged. Glen had always been able to read her like an open book.

"It's not important, Glen. Considering everything else that's happened . . ."

"Oh, but it is. After all, you did come rushing out here to try and help. My security isn't nearly as good as I thought. I just hope the reporters aren't half as clever."

He waited as the silence deepened between the two of them. But then, he was always good at waiting.

"I thought Janna Lawrence might be on board." Jo stopped, and finally rushed on in explanation. "She was on the ship with her staff before." Her voice ended on a defensive note.

"Janna? Not likely. She's back in New York. Planning her wedding."

Jo looked blank.

Glen grinned. "It seems she's fallen in love with my new division chief from England, Haywood Heath. He's in New York to begin overseeing the office there. Anyway, Woody and Janna took one look at each other and it was love at first sight! They've been inseparable ever since."

Jo's thoughts were in turmoil. Haywood Heath and Janna getting married . . .

"But New York? That's your territory, isn't it? I thought . . ."

Suddenly Glen was very close to her, dark, shimmering eyes looking into her own. "I recently had it on good authority that I spend too much time working and don't leave enough time for more important things, like my wife and family. So, I've decided to delegate. To Woody Heath."

Jo flushed. The words had been hers, only her tone had been considerably different.

Glen reached out a hand and ran it through her short, dark curls. "You know, I almost like your hair this way, now that I'm used to it. It suits you in a way, more . . . I don't know. Younger somehow?" His finger traced a familiar pattern over her cheek and down her throat.

"Glen, I . . ."

"You're not still worrying about Janna Lawrence, are you Josephine? You have no reason to. As attractive as you are, you have no reason to worry much about anybody. At least as far as I'm concerned."

Jo could feel herself being drawn closer by invisible bonds of familiarity that she suddenly knew she didn't want to shake off. She tilted her head upward, reaching toward Glen, as he took her wrist in his hand and tenderly kissed the inside.

A door slammed sharply down the hall and Sarah James appeared. She paused, her eyes taking in the scene.

"Jo! I'm glad I caught you. You left your purse on the couch!"

Glen had dropped his arms, but his eyes were still locked on Jo. She reluctantly turned away and went to collect her bag.

"Thanks again, Sarah. I'll call if I find out anything new."

Glen followed, an unreadable expression had returned to his face. He gave Jo a sidelong glance, his face half-masked in the shadows of the companionway.

"Call, even it you don't find out anything new. I mean, I'd like to hear from you."

Sarah looked quizzically at the pair as Jo mumbled in return: "I will. But I don't know if we've made that much progress this afternoon."

"Oh, I disagree. I think we've made all kinds of progress. About the murder, and otherwise!"

Then he smiled, that dazzling smile that Jo remembered from happier days; the smile that could make her forget what she was about to say and take her breath away all at the same time.

She was still considering Glen's last words, as Quint ran the surfboat up onto the beach, and Jo ran back through the gardens, attempting to escape the coming rain.

But there was no way she could escape her thoughts.

Chapter Seventeen

> Eternity was in our lips and eyes,
> —Shakespeare, *Antony and Cleopatra*

The sky was darkening with smoky-gray, phantom-like clouds as Jo drove slowly south on Route 64 to the causeway and home. The water in the sound had changed from a gorgeous, aquamarine color to a dull, armadillo gray, while the growing waves streaked toward the shore, casting milky-white foam high into the air. The wind smelled of the coming rain; the egrets squawked a warning, and Jo stepped harder on the accelerator, anxious to be inside before the storm reached land.

Jo pulled the Chevy into the parking lot of the Learned Owls just as two streaks of white-hot lightning turned the sea into a bubbly cauldron. She exited the car with more haste than grace, just as the first raindrops came pelting down.

"There you are! At last! The phone hasn't stopped ringing since you left!" Tara was busy making lemonade for the lounge area of the bookstore, while Marlowe was comfortably curled up behind the mystery section, snoring peacefully, regardless of the turbulent weather brewing outside.

"So who called?" Jo dumped her purse onto the couch,

sank down, and kicked off her wet shoes. Marlowe woke, gave her an inquiring look, and quickly went back to sleep.

Tara pulled a white slip of paper from the pocket of her jeans. "Cyn was first, only I couldn't understand her too well. She was on a cell phone, I think, and her voice was breaking up. But it sounded like she was inquiring about Glen and what was happening here."

Jo nodded absentmindedly. Cyn would be back in New York, where everything was larger than life and even the sounds were magnified into a pulsating roar. Jo thought of the soothing emerald green of the sea with the translucent early morning fog washing over the shoals and inlets, and concluded that she had the best of the deal.

"Okay. Call number two was your mother. She asked about Glen. Also, she wanted you to know she's going on an archaeological dig for the weekend in Arizona." Tara wrinkled up a well-defined nose. "No bathrooms or running water, right?"

"Right. My mother is a true pioneer and would have managed fine on a wagon train going west for California.

"Wagons ho! Anyway, she'll call when she returns."

"Call number three?"

"An obnoxious reporter wanting an interview with Mrs. Howard." Tara avoided Jo's gaze. "I just said there was no one by that name here."

"Good. You're doing fine, Tara. Keep going."

"Number four was the delectable Norman Switec. Again, about Glen. Seems he heard the news this morning at the aquarium. He would like you to give him a call." Tara looked at her with curiosity.

Jo hesitated. "Later, when I have some news. Nothing has happened except Glen's out on bail."

"Last, but hardly the least: Bobbi Partridge. And she sounded kind of strange and secretive!"

Jo slowly swung her feet down off the couch. "What did she say, exactly?"

"Evidently," and here Tara dropped her voice, "Possum left some sort of package or folder with her in the duplex. The package had your name on it. He seemed . . . rather excited and shook up. I can't imagine Possum excited or shook up."

"Neither can I. Hopefully it was something about the diary.

"Anyhow, she says if you want to take a looksee, she's at her parents' place up in Duck."

"Duck? Like up toward Corolla and the aquarium?"

"Where the delectable Norman feeds the fishes? Yep. She said," Tara looked expectantly at Jo, "she would be home this afternoon if you would like to call on her. Here are the directions." The assistant passed over a white piece of paper. "It's not hard. Duck isn't exactly large, if you know what I mean."

"Yeah, I know." Jo rubbed her eyes wearily and listened to the raindrops tapping on the roof like miniature dancing feet.

"It's wet outside," Tara said unnecessarily. "Not much you could do anyway. The store is quiet."

"And there's no reason why I shouldn't go."

"You know the old saying, the early bird gets the worm."

"Town of Duck, Bird Sanctuary," was the sign Jo spotted through the sheets of driving rain pounding off the hood of her car. Traveling north on Route 12, she had the road almost to herself. All the locals and tourists were staying inside because of the weather, Jo thought gloomily to herself. Even the blasted ducks and other species of birds inhabiting the region had sense enough to get in out of the downpour.

She fumbled with the directions to Bobbi's home on Scarbough Lane. "North of town on the right-hand turnoff from Duck Drive." Jo peered through the steam on her windshield. Vacation cottages and beach rentals met her gaze along with the water-splattered sand dunes and miles of ocean grasses.

Soon she reached the middle of town and the peace and quiet vanished. A collection of shops and sports centers were crowded into a brief, one-mile area. Signs advertising jet ski rentals, parasailing, kayaking—plus tarner activities such as sailing and fishing—were arranged one on top of another. A bike path, called the Duck Trail, was used for recreation, and a sign asked drivers to "Be Careful, Be Courteous, Be Safe," of bikers and hikers, currently non-existent due to the rain.

Jo found the turnoff toward the sea, as she zigged and zagged over a half-flooded road. There were only a few houses on the Atlantic side of the street; all were raised up on stilts with the front porches ten feet above ground level to avoid the rising water. Bobbi's blue-slated, three-steepled home by the turnaround was easy to locate. Jo parked the car and made a run up the stairs to the porch enclosing the front of the house. Bobbi had a typical shell garden out front. A tiny yellow parakeet twittered in a cage by an open window on the first floor. Jo straightened up and looked back toward the Atlantic; the volatile sea was shooting bolts of white foam high up onto the beach. The two trees out front looked scoured by the weather, with drooping leaves and hanging branches.

Jo flattened her collar on the light jacket she wore and rapped on the door. It was opened, almost instantaneously, by Bobbi Partridge, who must have seen Jo's Chevy pull in.

Jo eased through the ornate, dark-wooded doorway. Her shoes squished down the hallway as Bobbi directed her into the main parlor. Jo's jaw dropped as she entered the room, with its clash of bright, harlequin colors and theatre posters of Bobbi Partridge throughout different stages of her career.

Bobbi motioned Jo to the dove-blue sofa with bright red accessories, including a fringed, red lamp on a nearby table. She sank down in the chair opposite, almost as though her legs were too weak to hold her upright.

Bobbi seemed to have aged twenty years overnight. Even the heavy makeup she wore did not conceal the dark rings under her eyes, or the trembling of her fingers as she lit a cigarette from one already burning in an ashtray.

"I know it's a little much," Bobbi indicated the posters and neon brillance of the room, "but my parents have always been my most dedicated fans. I think my dad has seen every play I've ever been in."

"They have a right to be proud. You've been quite successful."

Bobbi stared at the glowing end of her cigarette. Then she gave a harsh, crackling laugh that turned into a choking cough.

"I think I got lucky. I'm not . . . brilliant. I'm not even very pretty." She waved an arm negligently in Jo's direction when the younger woman opened her mouth to object.

"I'm nothing but a third-rate actress who ended up in a little tourist town in North Carolina, when she couldn't hack it in Hollywood. I'm almost fifty years old, Jo," she said with a sigh.

She leaned her head back against the sofa. Jo held her tongue and waited. Long minutes dragged by before Bobbi Partridge raised her head.

"But Possum saw something different. He was twenty years older, but, my God, he saw something beautiful. He thought I was beautiful. And the strangest thing happened. I felt that way when we were together. He was the most important person in my world, and now he's gone forever."

Jo's heart went out to the woman. "He lit up when he mentioned your name."

Her grief was like some physical thing that was now washing over her like the tide lapping the shore.

"I searched my whole life for somebody like Possum. And I found him here. We only had a year. I don't think I had even begun to appreciate what we had. I never told him, Jo, what he meant to me. I never told him! And now it's too late and he's gone!"

Jo shifted awkwardly on the sofa. The pain of others always made her uncomfortable, mainly because she never knew what to say to help ease it.

"He knew, Bobbi," Jo said slowly. "Possum was a wise man and he realized you loved him. People don't always have to have it spelled out for them, they just know."

Bobbi pulled a wilted-looking paper towel out of the baggy sweater she wore and wiped her eyes.

"Did he, Jo? I hope so. Because if I had it to do again, I would tell Possum how much I loved him every hour of every day. If I had known . . . but I thought we had years left, when we really had only minutes . . ."

She turned her head down, rather like an animal shielding itself from some sort of torment. "I was so difficult sometimes with him. But he stuck it out. And I . . . I never told him."

Her eyes closed as two gigantic tears made furrows down the makeup on her face. They glistened in the light of the fringed lamp before falling onto her jeans.

A sudden snap of lightening, followed by thunder out on the ocean, made her wonder if Bobbi's heart hadn't broken in two.

"If you ever find somebody that loves you like that, Jo, don't ever let him go. Hang on to him for all you're worth. Most people, the lucky ones, only find him maybe once. Don't lose him, the way I did."

She wiped her nose again on the grimy paper towel and shoved it back up her sleeve.

"Had you quarreled with him, then?" Jo asked softly.

"No. It was impossible to quarrel with Possum. To fight. I tried, though." The harsh laugh sounded again. "I was insensitive, stupid, jealous, when I saw you with him."

"Of me? But why? I'm not famous, an actress. I'm so ordinary . . ."

"Never. You are unique. Something in your eyes. I always go by the eyes. They are a mirror to the soul." She hiccuped. "I can't remember who said that. Don't suppose it matters much."

"If there's anything I can do for you . . ."

"For me?" She looked at Jo, as though considering the question. "Can you bring him back to me? Can you bring my Possum back from the dead?"

Jo shook her head, almost sorry that she had asked.

"I feel a real crying binge coming on. You'd better take this. Possum left it in the duplex before he was killed. For you. I don't know what it is and I don't think I especially care."

She shoved a manila folder across the table. Jo picked it up and glanced inside.

"Photographs. And the diary. Bobbi, thank you. And I hope things get better for you. If the police find who's responsible . . ."

"It still won't bring Possum back. Nothing can." She rose unsteadily from the sofa. "If you'll excuse me . . ."

"Of course." Jo grabbed her purse and moved toward the door. The little canary in his cage gave a few mournful chirps as she passed.

"Remember what I said, Jo. Once you have found him, never let him go. That came from *South Pacific*. Ezio Pinza and Mary Martin, over fifty years ago. I never made it to Broadway, either," she added as though to forestall Jo's question. "Possum told me he saw that play years ago. It's good advice."

"Yes," Jo said softly. "It's very good advice."

Chapter Eighteen

'Will you walk into my parlor?'
said the Spider to the Fly;
'Tis the prettiest little parlor
that ever you did spy.'
—Mary Howitt, *The Spider and the Fly*

The rain was still pouring down as Jo maneuvered the Chevy back toward the main town of Duck, over a flooded Scarbough Lane. A mournful heron flopped in one of the pink-flowering crepe myrtle trees that dotted the road at periodic intervals. Jo reached the cutoff and pulled over into a clear area. She fumbled into her purse, grasped the cell phone nestled toward the bottom, and dragged it out. Her gaze returned to the folder.

"To hell with it," Jo muttered aloud. "I've traveled all over the Outer Banks, even to Barbados, to find the answer to Cristabel and her diary. I want to know now!"

Jo leaned back in her seat as the rain beat a tattoo on the hood of the car. She opened the folder and studied the first picture.

The photographs were black and white, some were lithographs; all were very old and definitely taken a long time ago. The pictures seemed to be of basically the same area, a forest with a grove of trees and some level ground in front. The trees could be machineel; they were the right height and it looked like little half-rotted piles of spoiled fruit lay on the ground close by.

But where? Jo frowned thoughtfully. There was no sign, no marker, no nothing! She sighed and rubbed her eyes and then opened the diary. A note written on blue notepaper fell out.

Possum's words filled the car, almost as though he were sitting next to her.

Sorry about the paper. Blue is Bobbi's favorite color. Fact is, I had a feeling of trouble after you went. So, I left the diary and the pictures with Bobbi, up at her place. No, I don't recognize the site of the black and white photographs. But I got to looking at the leather binding on the diary. Books and book-binding kind of went together, at least back when I first got into the trade. Anyway, inside the back slip-cover was a hidden pocket. Cristabel must have used it after she was married and had a child. There was a drawing in pen and ink. Our Cristabel was quite an artist. I assume the man was her husband and the child her son. The problem I have is that their picture doesn't remind me of anyone, any more than the black and white photographs did. Perhaps you'll have better luck. I'm going to run this letter, the photographs, and the diary up to Bobbi's place now. Call it an old man's heebee-jeebies, but I have a very nasty feeling about all of this.

Be careful. I wish I could do more to help you, since I've always loved you like a daughter.

Possum

Jo felt the tears forming behind her eyelids as she carefully removed the artist's sketch from under the back flyleaf and stared at the picture. A young black man and a child stared back at her. The artist had depicted close-ups of the two faces, with the man dressed in farmer's work clothes and the child in dark-colored overalls.

Jo looked closely at the picture. There was something so familiar about it. She took a white piece of paper from her purse, tore a hole in it, and put the paper over one figure and then the other, with just the face showing through.

And suddenly she knew! The long, narrow jaw of the man, the full lips and protruding ebony eyes that seemed, even in a hand-drawn picture, to capture the souls of the subjects. Possum was right. Cristabel had been quite an artist. Or perhaps because these two people had been the loves of her life, she had caught their essence in a way that nobody else on the earth would have been able to do.

Jo hesitated and then reached for her cell phone and dialed Norman Switec's number at the aquarium.

"Jo! Great to hear from you!" Norm's voice boomed heartily out. "I heard about Possum. So sorry."

Hurriedly Jo explained to Norm about Possum leaving the diary and pictures of the treasure location with Bobbi. "I'm already in Duck with the water rising in the road. I was wondering if you would be interested in having a look. I could just keep going north. It's not far, but with this infernal rain, it's going to take awhile."

Jo caught the interest in Norm's voice when he spoke. "Sure. Come on up. The rain has certainly kept the tourists away. It's bad, even on the sound. I'd be happy to give those pictures a look."

"Great! I'm on my way!" Jo hung up and then dialed Tara Cataldo at the bookstore.

"Jo! Have you heard? The road just washed out north of the Route 158 turnoff. And it's raining cats and dogs here." A long pause followed. "Er . . . you know what I mean. No reflection on Marlowe, of course."

"That means," Jo said slowly, "I might not get back tonight." She paused. "Tara, I picked up some pictures that Possum left with Bobbi, plus a family sketch that Cristabel did. But I still can't identify where the photographs were taken. The trees look like her descriptions of the poison trees. Anyway, I'm going up to Corolla to see Norm at the aquarium. Next to Possum, he knows more about the area than anyone else around; he's explored every inch of these shoals and inlets. He may know the location. And if the treasure can be found . . ."

There was a stillness at the other end of the line. "Jo, I'm not sure that this is such a great idea. With the road washed out, you're kind of stranded up there."

"But I thought you liked 'the delectable Norman.' What's happened? I'm just going to talk to the man, drive back down to one of the bed and breakfasts off of Route 12, and hole up until the water goes down."

The silence on the other end of the line lengthened. "I just have a bad feeling about it, that's all."

Jo tried a half-laugh. "Tara, you're worrying over nothing. Norm is a respected member of the marine community and just trying to help out!"

"You take care, Jo. Marlowe and I will be waiting when you get back."

Tara disconnected quickly, almost as though she had something else she suddenly had to do. Or someone else she had to call?

Jo felt clammy sweat break out on her palms. "This is ridiculous," she said aloud. It was as if Tara's paranoia was catching, like the measles. Jo slid the cell phone back into her purse and slowly, thoughtfully, turned the car north toward Corolla.

The rain came down even harder, plastering flowery blossoms to trees and forcing branches across the road. Fortunately, the aquarium was on the inside of the long, protruding finger of the Northern Outer Banks. Jo didn't even want to think what the Atlantic side of Corolla would be like in this weather.

She peered ahead. A number of small boats bobbed at piers by the edge of the sound. Large, dark clouds gathered, swirling around like some sort of defiled beast farther out over the water, as the road zigged and zagged ever northward toward Corolla.

Eventually Jo came upon the brick lighthouse guarding the shore. She gave a gasp of relief as she pulled into the parking lot surrounding the white and yellow, multi-layered aquarium. The place was certainly deserted, not one car remained, despite the relatively early hour. Jo grasped her purse and the manila folder. She pulled the diary and Cristabel's sketch out of the envelope and dropped them into the pocket of her jacket, then she waited patiently for a break in the downpour before running helter-skelter for the main entrance.

The surf-boat bobbed in the storm, its main mast saluted her as she tore past. Finally she was inside the building, listening to the fury of the rain exhaust itself on the glass roof, while soothing sounds of the sea were piped in over the speaker system of the aquarium.

The place had a morose feeling to it with no children or even adults wandering around, peering into the exhibits or looking at the environmental films in Neptune's Theatre. Her feet made odd, hollow noises on the wooden flooring as Jo slid past the darkened gift shop and into the ladies room to repair the rain damage to her hair and makeup.

Jo ran a comb through her short, dark hair. She peeked out at the weather. Looking toward the back of the building, Jo could see a forest of masts swaying at a nearby pier. Then her eyes focused on the two cars parked discreetly behind several storm-tossed trees. One was the utility vehicle belonging to the aquarium and used by Norm. As she stared at the other car, Jo felt her breath catch in her throat.

It was a dark green Mercedes with personalized New York license plates. The designer plates were familiar, as they should be, since she and Glen Howard had selected them right after their marriage: *Ho-Jo,* for the publishing company which bore both their names. There could be no mistake.

Jo closed her eyes and willed the car to be gone, but it was no use. The green Mercedes with the damning plates was still there.

Jo leaned her head wearily against the wall. Glen was in the building with Norm. Waiting for what? For her? To deliver the manila folder with the pictures that Possum had left? And do what? Had Norm called on Possum after Tara had innocently told the fish expert that Jo had gone to see the old man and demanded the information? And had one or the other—or even both—killed him when he refused?

"Oh, Glen, why? You have so much! We have so much!" Jo thought back to everything they owned; the publishing empire, the houses, cars, influence, power. Glen had wanted more. And he had found a willing accomplice in Norman Switec.

Jo slowly eased back out of the bathroom. She had to get away, get back out to her car and drive somewhere—in spite of the flooded roads and the rain and the high water—before the two men killed her, too. Glen and Norm. The love she had begun to feel again for Glen turned to burnt ash in her heart. She had to get away and now!

Jo stole quietly back down the hallway toward the blinking sign marked "Exit," toward the parking lot. She heard stealthy footsteps as she eased into the final turn past the gift shop.

"Jo!" Norman Switec's voice boomed out in the quiet corridor. "I didn't hear you come in! Why you're drenched! Come back to my office and have some coffee. And I can check out those photographs while you're there."

Not on your life, Jo thought silently. Or mine either! She racked her brain for any excuse to get out of the building. But Norman was blocking the main exit and coming closer by the minute, his mannequin smile plastered into place.

Forget the excuse! Jo bolted back down the corridor, the manila folder clutched desperately to her chest. She reached the corner and turned. Norm was following, but much slower. Jo scooted into the wreck exhibit surrounding the "Graveyard of the Atlantic" display and stopped on the far side of the room, palms sweating, a lump in her throat. She looked overhead as the dark shadows in the shark tank gave her an idea.

She walked backward, kitty-corner to the restroom, and almost collided with Norm as he was creeping along the far side. He gave a surprised yell as Jo came down hard on his instep and kept going, past the theatre and the wetlands exhibit to the shark tank.

Norm was thundering along in her wake, cursing loudly, as she turned and ran up the stairs toward the catwalk.

Jo reached the skytop level under the glassed-in roof and groaned. The catwalk was still being repaired, with the sign "Danger-Keep Off" displayed prominently across the deck, backed by a chain to stop unauthorized access. It wouldn't be possible for her to cross and run down the stairs on the other side.

Jo stopped, her back against the chain as Norm wheezed up the stairs, sounding like he had asthma. Then her ears detected a second set of footsteps treading lightly behind him.

She turned and broke through the tacky, little chain and out onto the catwalk. It swayed rather like a suspension bridge hanging in the air. Below, the water looked opaque in the semi-light, with ugly, deformed fins breaking the surface at odd intervals. Jo's mind flashed to the razor-sharp teeth on the beasts. Glancing down, it seemed to her that the fins were beginning to circle, as though the sharks were waiting for her to tumble—or be shoved—into the pool. Jo crowded against the railing, feeling like a mouse in a trap, as Norman Switec puffed to the top of the stairs.

He stood illuminated against the glassed-in panels of the aquarium; behind his silhouetted form, the rain tumbled down and the sky and sea turned black. No words were necessary between the two of them, their relationship was clear: the hunter and the hunted. Below, the shark fins circled faster in the nebulous murk of the dark water.

Norm spoke calmly, quietly, as though out for a day of fishing on the Currituck Sound.

"Come on Jo, give it up. Just let me have the manila folder. That's what I really want. And we can crawl back down from here and go home."

For a moment, Jo wanted to believe him. She felt a flood of despair begin to seep through her. What was the use in fighting any more? Glen was here, apparently partners with Norm in his crimes. The car had been parked outside, plain as could be. She stared down into the churning water, feeling sick to her stomach and slightly dizzy.

She shifted uncomfortably on her perch. The suspension bridge swayed slowly. Jo wondered how much longer it was going to hold.

Norm inched forward, causing the catwalk to shudder. His eyes shifted downward, almost subconsciously, as he held out his hand.

Jo pulled back. Norm's face darkened.

"Let me have the folder, Jo. Make this easy on both of us."

"Why? So you can kill me too?"

Norm's eyes glistened in the half-light from the windows. A crackling flash of yellow lightning made them gleam like those of a fox stalking his prey.

"They deserved to die. Watson Wise for mocking Blackbeard, and Possum for refusing to help me with the diary. I knew about it, you see. My grandmother had some letters and papers. When she died, I went through the lot. One of the letters told of the diary, but that was all. That's why *I'm* entitled to the treasure. Me and nobody else. Because nobody else has a direct connection to Blackbeard!"

"Norm, there's something you need to know." Jo licked her lips. Would he believe what she felt in her soul to be true? That he was not a direct descendent of Blackbeard? Jo felt for a moment like she was talking with a madman, as Norm shifted his weight and came closer. He seemed strangely oblivious to the danger on the catwalk.

"Hand over that folder, Jo. Let's see what Possum Slocum was willing to die for."

Jo leaned back slightly. Lightning flared once more across the sky. Norm's gaze turned upward. Then Jo heard the sound of footsteps coming up the stairs to the bridge.

Of course Glen would be coming. He would want to be in on the kill. Her husband would never want to be deprived of that.

Jo felt sick to her stomach. The footsteps sounded louder on the stairway.

Norm frowned. He half-turned to the figure that stood shadowed in the glow of lightning. Then darkness shrouded the catwalk as the power went out.

There was still enough light to barely illuminate the bridge. Finally the emergency lighting blazed on. Jo had inched forward, but stopped and hastily retreated back to her precarious perch on the catwalk.

"You haven't told me about your partner, Norm. What was Glen's part in all of this? He can hardly claim to be related to Blackbeard. And he surely doesn't need the money."

Jo's gaze went to the figure bound in shadow. Norm gave a puzzled sigh as a third voice spoke out. A woman's voice.

"What in the hell makes you think that his partner was Glen Howard?" And Cynthia Savene moved to join Norman Switec at the far edge of the catwalk.

Chapter Nineteen

Fair is foul, and foul is fair;
Hover through the fog and filthy air.
            —Shakespeare, *MacBeth*

Jo felt as though she were moving slowly through a nightmare, as the shock of her best friend's appearance began to register in her mind. Then a glorious, golden warmth seeped through her chilled soul. Glen hadn't been involved at all! He was innocent! Suddenly she felt able to move again, to resist, to think. Hope coursed through her body like liquid brandy, setting it on fire.

Cyn smiled nastily. "I can't believe you had no idea."

"But why, Cyn? You're hardly a relation to Blackbeard. And . . . murder?"

Norm laughed heartily, but it soon dissolved into a rather high-pitched giggle. "Can't you figure it out, Jo? Cyn got tired of being the best friend looking for handouts. She wanted the money from the treasure as badly as I did. One husband after another and just no luck. Or cash, I should say. She had to beg for every last cent. Even Glen. The only thing she ever got from him, I gather, was the loan of his car. So typical with a loser like her!"

"Shut up, Norm. You talk too much. Just get those photographs if you ever want to find the loot!"

The man had fallen back a few steps. Jo realized her best

bet was to keep Cyn and Norm talking. The partners seemed to be close to a major falling out. Instinctively Jo knew to encourage it.

"So it was money? This whole thing is about money?"

"Only a person who has always had it could make a statement like that," Cyn spat viciously. "You had everything I ever wanted! And you never seemed to even care!"

Jo spoke slowly. "So you were so jealous that you what? Tried to kill me with two accidents?"

"Three accidents! Only the last two weren't meant to kill you. We wanted you to lead us to the treasure. Only this idiot screwed up," Cyn ended in disgust.

"But you said three accidents?" Jo spoke very slowly.

Cyn laughed then, her face a contorted mask. "I knew you were quick. Can't you figure it out, a bright, little witch like you?"

Jo thought back to the New York apartment and the bannister that had given way. And Cyn had been so close, so conveniently close.

Jo's face blanched. "My baby. You killed my baby!" Her mind flashed to that time, remembering the long months when she had alternately blamed first herself and then Glen, for not being there when she needed him. And the fault rested with neither of them. It had been Cyn! Cyn staying over, sympathizing, being so kind, so loving, planting seeds of doubt about Glen, about herself. Jo felt a sick wave of nausea flow over her. It had been her best friend. Her baby was dead, her husband alienated from her. Jo felt herself shaking like a cornered animal. She was alone and unloved, because of Cyn.

Jo closed her eyes, as something akin to anger began burning like a tiny flame deep in her gut. A flame that she fanned into white-hot fury.

Jo opened her eyes and glanced down. The manila folder was still in her hand; the diary and Cristabel's sketch still in her jacket pocket. And the catwalk still swayed underneath her in the open space like a horse bucking and kicking, while below, the fins of the sharks continued to circle.

Jo licked her lips and stared, first at Cyn, and finally at Norm. If she was going to die, it wouldn't be easily.

Jo slowly backed further out on the catwalk.

"You want this folder?" Jo could almost see Norm licking his lips. "You really want it? The location of Blackbeard's treasure? Well, come and get it!"

And she held out her arm, her fingers clutching the folder tightly, over the shark pool.

"No!" Norm shrieked, sounding like a woman in pain.

"Get out there and stop her, Norm!" Cyn ordered calmly. "She's bluffing. She won't drop it. Jo wants to find out where that treasure is as badly as we do."

Norm paused, then grasped Cyn's arm and dragged her forward. The catwalk swung dangerously from side to side. Cyn's eyes widened.

"What are you doing?" Her voice rose to a high, shrill whine as she twisted in his grasp.

"If I'm going down, you're coming with me!"

Cyn pulled away frantically, causing the wires holding the catwalk to spark with electricity.

Jo laughed. "You're smarter than you look, Norm. Why should she have everything her way?"

She waved the manila folder out in front of her.

"Back off now, Norm. And take her with you. Or I'm going to start dropping these down to our little finny friends. Maybe *they'll* have fun looking at them. And you'll never find Blackbeards' treasure. Not that you're entitled to it anyway. You're no relation at all! And I can prove it!"

In the distance there was the dull thud of thunder rocketing across the water.

"What do you mean, Jo? Or is this just more lies?"

"No, not this time. Take a look at this sketch. Possum found it under the flyleaf of Cristabel's diary. She sketched her husband and son. Now you look closer and tell me who the child reminds you of?" Jo yanked the picture from her jacket pocket and wiggled it tantalizingly in front of Norm's face.

"Good Norm. Come take a looksee."

He snatched the sketch from her hand. Cyn stopped trying to pull away and squinted over his shoulder. She
reached for the sketch, but Norm swatted angrily at her
hand, rather like she was a fly who wouldn't go away.

"Now you tell me if Cristabel's husband and child don't
remind you of someone. The same cheekbones, the same
protruding eyes and mouth. It's the face you see in the
mirror every morning. The child looks enough like you to
be your twin." Jo balanced herself delicately on the catwalk. "Might even have the same buck teeth. And if you're
related to Cristabel's son, you certainly couldn't be related
to Blackbeard." Jo smiled smugly. "As Cristabel would say,
Comprenez-vous, Norm?"

Norm's face had turned a deadly white color. He studied
the picture, his body beginning to tremble.

Jo laughed. "The light has dawned! Cristabel speaks
from the grave and gives us her last message. *And* wins the
final round, so to speak, in spite of everything!"

Jo leaned back, ensconced on her portion of the catwalk.
She could hear another crack of lightning across the sound.
And a different noise that Jo barely recognized. It sounded
like the motor of an expensive, high-powered engine, coming closer and very fast.

Cyn looked at the picture. "No, Norm! She's lying! Listen to me! The witch will say anything. Use your common
sense for God's sake! How can you be so stupid? And what
difference does it make anyway?"

"What difference does it make? It's my life, my soul.
Cristabel's son! I thought there was a direct line . . ." His
voice dropped to a sick whisper. "What I've done . . . when
I think of what I've done . . ."

Jo saw his face break out in a dark sheen as he continued
to mumble, "Not related? My whole life . . ."

"You damned fool. What difference can it make?" Cyn
repeated again. Spittle flecked from her mouth. "The treasure is what's important, not that imbecile of a pirate. Think
of the money, Norm! Enough to do whatever you want, go
wherever you want, never to have to consider another human being . . ."

Norm looked at Cyn for a long moment, rather like a mongoose staring down a cobra. "It was just the money with you. And the revenge. But for me . . . Blackbeard was my life! My soul! The greatest pirate of them all!"

Cyn licked her lips nervously as Norm swayed back-and-forth on the catwalk like a drunken man. And then he screamed, like a wounded animal in terrible pain. His whimpering continued, saliva running from between his lips, as he reached out almost blindly. The bridge beneath the three of them swung dangerously, back and forth. Jo looked into Norman Switec's face. For a second, he reminded her of his namesake in *Psycho,* eyes bright with maniacal fury.

"My whole life—destroyed."

Norm, with Cyn in his grasp, was three-quarters of the way off the catwalk. Cyn was twisting wildly, trying to drag herself back to the platform and safety. But Norman Switec's strength was that of a crazy person and she couldn't break away.

Jo heard the guide wires on the catwalk snap, the black iron tip striking her shoulder, throwing her sideways. She clung to the edge with one hand as Cyn turned to her and screamed piteously.

"Jo, help me! Please, in the name of God, help me!"

She should stop him, Jo thought. But how? She couldn't move past the guide wires. And then she thought once more of Possum; kindly old Possum, who had treated her more like an adopted, beloved daughter than as a Northern stranger who'd purchased his bookstore. And she thought of Bobbi Partridge with her swollen, tear-soaked face. And her own baby?

"Jo, don't just stand there. Do something! Please!"

She tried to move, but it was too late, as Norm slammed Cyn back against the guide wires. Then he linked his arm with hers and stepped silently over the side, dragging her in his wake.

Jo blinked hard. When she opened her eyes, the catwalk was empty except for herself. The envelope with the photographs was gone, lost over the side. Jo peered below; the water was covered with white bloody foam, as the sharks had their after-dinner dessert.

The release of Norm and Cyn's weight swung the cat-walk back around, as Jo half-walked, half-dragged herself toward the stair-well. She saw two figures hurriedly detach themselves from the shadows. Jo bit her lip against the pain seeping through her shoulder and hauled herself the last few feet into Glen Howard's arms.

As he crushed her against himself, sobbed against her cheek. "I thought we weren't going to be in time. I thought . . ."

Jo buried her face against his coat as the second shadowy figure frantically started punching numbers into his cell phone.

"Detective Wolfe," Jo murmured weakly. "Let me guess. You're telling them you are working on it!"

Wolfe detached himself from the phone. "Oh no, Mrs. Howard. According to my verbal report, I've solved it!"

Chapter Twenty

A sight to dream of, not to tell!
—Samuel Taylor Coleridge, *Cristabel*

Gusts of wind swooped past the wharf where the dive boat had been temporarily docked. Jo could see police officers swarming like miniature ants across the gunwale, down the gangplank, and into the aquarium. High overhead, the phantom-black clouds were beginning to dissipate, revealing pale, icy-looking stars glittering down. The smell of salt was in the air from the storm-tossed sea, as the waves washed up on the beach, where the forty-four-foot surfboat was moored against the pier. Jo studied it thoughtfully from her bed in Glen's suite overlooking the inlet. Her right arm and shoulder were draped in white bandages, which the doctor from the dive boat had hastily applied.

"They were going to get the photos and then kill me and dump my body into the inlet using the surfboat." Jo could feel the sweat breaking out and coursing over her new bandages.

"Probably." Glen sat at the foot of the bed, holding her unbandaged hand. Jo turned from her study of the activity outside the suite's window.

"But how did you know? I mean, to come here? I wasn't even vaguely suspicious of Norm! Or Cyn either!"

"Actually, the story begins when you were down in Barbados. I felt that you were becoming a bit ... er ... accident prone after what happened on the *Queen Anne's Revenge* during the dive. Then there was the accident to Watson Wise that wasn't an accident at all. At any rate, when you checked in to my resort ..."

"The Palm Terrace is yours? And the beach house, too?" Jo leaned back weakly.

"I had to do something, Josephine. You didn't want me around after what happened on the *Queen Anne's Revenge*. So I finagled your staying at the Palm Terrace. Of course, I never realized that Cyn was the enemy." He sighed wearily. "I tried to make you safe, and ended up putting you with the most dangerous person of all."

"Tried to make me safe?"

Glen grinned. "What did you think of Octavia and Michael?"

"They worked for you?"

Glen nodded. "Also that poor soul who spent his time hacking off the hotel's begonias and poinciana trees. He's really security in disguise."

"Octavia and the rest. You ... went through so much trouble!"

"But it was almost for nothing. When Tara Cataldo called ..."

"Tara! Does she work for you, too?"

"No, she just likes happy endings. Something about reading the end of a book before the beginning." He paused. "I should try that sometime. Maybe it would be an improvement."

"But Tara?" Jo prompted.

"Tara had my number from all the times I called the bookstore. Fortunately, when you said you were going up to see "the delectable Norm," as she put it, with those photographs, and the road washed out, well, she got nervous. Gave me a call on the dive boat."

"And you floated to the rescue. Along with the local police."

"Yes. Luckily I'd had the dive boat refitted. Anyway, I'd called Detective Wolfe on my cell phone. He had been increasingly suspicious of Norman Switec. The fellow wasn't that hard to persuade, actually. Wolfe notified the local authorities and came along. Then . . ." Glen's voice faltered, "I thought we were too late."

"No, you were just in time." Jo traced a design on her white arm bandage. "But . . ."

"But what, Josephine?"

"They killed so many people. Possum, Watson Wise, and . . . my baby. Cyn caused my accident in New York. And they let me lead them toward the treasure. They were watching in the bookstore and in Barbados. Cyn rigged the elevator so I would stay over at the Palm Terrace longer. It gave Norm more of a chance to look around and find the diary."

"And Norm pushed Watson Wise over the side of the dive boat, lifted my Rolex, and tried to hang Possum's murder on me!"

"You lent Cyn your car?"

"Yes. She was your best friend and was whining about not having any way to drive down to visit. I should have told her to take a plane, like everyone else!"

"It was all for nothing," Jo said slowly. "When Norm found out he wasn't related to Blackbeard, he just went crazy."

"Lucky for you he did. Otherwise you would have been shark dessert instead of Norm and Cyn."

She shuddered and pressed close to him.

"Don't think about it anymore. It's over and done with."

"Except for finding the treasure, but the photographs are gone!"

"I already have my treasure," Glen murmured softly. "Let Blackbeard keep his!"

There was a sharp rap on the door of the suite. A second later, Detective Wolfe stuck an inquiring head around the corner.

"Just checking to see how you were doing, Mrs. Howard. You seemed a bit peaked."

Jo half-smiled as Glen stirred by her shoulder. "I'm much better now. Thank you, Detective."

Glen gave Wolfe a sharp glance. "You recovered the bodies?"

"Yes. Actually, Mrs. Savene drowned. Her lungs were full of water."

Glen turned to Josephine. "The sharks couldn't stomach her either, I guess." Then seeing his wife's look of distress, he fell silent.

Wolfe continued. "Norman Switec was practically torn in two. We tried to save his life, but it was no use." The man paused and looked at them rather like the cat that had swallowed the canary. "But I wanted to tell you," he turned to Jo. "You were right! Norman Switec was no long-lost relation of Blackbeard. We have positive proof!"

Jo looked at him quizzically.

"The doc ran some tests on his blood. There was enough spilled before he died. It seems he had sickle cell disease."

"Sickle cell?" Glen looked blank. "What's that?"

Wolfe yanked out a notebook from his overcoat pocket. "Sickle cell is a disease of anemia in the red blood cells of the human body," he stated in professional tones. "Red blood cells become hard and unwieldy going through the arteries and veins. They change shape. The disease is inherited from one generation to another and is normally found in Black Americans."

Jo narrowed her eyes in thought. "Norm did have episodes of pain and ulcers. He was always telling me about one thing or another that was wrong with him."

Wolfe added, "These are all symptoms of the disease. Also, it may have affected him mentally and indirectly cause his suicide."

"So his entire existence was built on a fallacy. The fallacy of his birth," Glen Howard concluded. "Such an obsession. To kill for photographs that might not have given him the lead he was seeking. He thought he was entitled to the treasure. That wasn't the case."

"The poison tree—" Jo interjected. "It truly poisoned Switec's mind." She leaned back in the bed and found a more comfortable position. "So were you surprised by the fact that Cyn and Norm were partners?"

Wolfe leaned back against the door. "No, actually not. I had suspected some connection between the two for quite some time. I'd had extensive background checks run on both of them. Some rather incriminating things turned up."

"You really did get your man, then. And woman."

Wolfe nodded and eased toward the door. "It's hardly surprising, you know."

Jo raised her brows in silent interrogation.

"Mrs. Savene's maiden name was Fox, wasn't it?"

"Yes. She changed it after her first marriage and for some reason kept the Savene. Must have liked the sound, I guess." Jo shrugged.

"Wasn't there some fable about a fox and a wolf? Aesop, perhaps? Anyway, didn't the fox lose out to the clever wolf and get eaten at the end?"

"I've never heard anything like that," Glen Howard muttered.

Jo merely looked blank.

"Well, if there wasn't," Detective Wolfe said smugly, "there surely should have been!"

And with a sly grin, he silently exited and closed the door behind him.

Chapter Twenty-One

And into my garden stole
When the night had veiled the pole;
In the morning glad I see
My foe outstretched beneath the tree
    —William Blake, *A Poison Tree*

T he sky was an overcast, gray mosaic on the day that
Norman Switec was laid to rest. Jo, with Glen at her side,
watched as the mahogany casket was lowered down to its
final resting place. Norman's body, or what was left of it,
had been handed over to the undertaker the previous day.
Now, bitter sea wind shifted and flowed around the oak
trees bordering the small cemetery, which was adjacent to
the white, clapboard church, located in Wanchese.

Jo pulled her sweater tightly over the bandages still cov-
ering her arm. The day was surprisingly cool for summer
off the North Carolina capes. As the reverend intoned final
words and sprinkled holy water over the casket, Jo closed
her eyes and tried to remember Norm in a positive light,
as a lover and protector of animals, and as someone who
truly appreciated the beauty of the earth and who fought
against anyone who tried to take that beauty away.

Jo realized that Norm's mind had snapped at the end,
due to his obsession with the heathen pirate Blackbeard and
no doubt helped along by Cyn and her rapacious lust for

the treasure. Jo thought back to the day she had climbed the Currituck Lighthouse steps and Norm had taken her to lunch at the Whalehead Club. The happy time, Jo thought sadly, before his obsession had destroyed his mind and caused his suicide.

The cemetery was empty. Old Mother Hibbard, who made a hobby of going to the graveside services was there, but aside from Jo and Glen and Father Morrison, there were no other mourners. Glen had murmured to Jo about her generosity in attending. Jo found it far easier to mourn for Norman Switec than for Cyn, who had been buried in New York the previous day.

Her mother had called with the news of Cyn's burial after Jo gave her a very abbreviated account of what had happened. Mrs. Sharpe's reply was typical and straight to the point.

"It doesn't surprise me, Jo. Why, when you and Cyn were younger, she always wanted your toys to play with. It was obvious when I used to watch the two of you together. And when she got them, well, Cyn would move on to something else and lose interest literally overnight. I guess she really didn't change that much as she got older. She just went from toys to men and money, that's all."

Jo shuddered as the cooling wind crept over her. Glen's arm tightened lovingly on her good shoulder. He had been with her constantly since her near fatal aquarium accident, running Ho-Jo Publications through long distance teleconferences and fax machine messages. Janna Lawrence and Woody Heath, Glen's new New York manager, would be getting married in the fall, and her husband talked of turning even more of the business over to him at that time.

Jo's attention returned to the Reverend Father Morrison, who was winding down with a prayer over Norman Switec's casket. What a dreary place, Jo thought uneasily. Brooding, short-trunked trees bordered the last row of cemetery lots, while a murky stream slithered over rocks farther back in the woods.

The reverend finished his final prayer and turned away to express condolences to the mourners. Mother Hibbard ambled away, scratching at some mosquito bites on her arm. Jo slipped into the high-vaulted church doorway and followed some stone steps down to the basement lavatory.

The church was old and the main altar had been built when the original village of Wanchese had been founded, shortly after the settlement at Manteo. Fresh fish would have been the main attraction then, as now. Regardless, Old Wharf Road, which bordered the church, wasn't much more than the dirt path it had been back in the eighteen-hundreds.

The basement was damp and had the musty smell frequently associated with an older structure. The walls had been whitewashed, possibly as someone's penance. Early scenes of the church had been hung unframed along the passage to the lavatory in an attempt at decoration.

Jo paused, her eyes focusing on one black and white sketch. The scene looked vaguely familiar with thirty-foot trees hovering in the background over a series of old-fashioned gravestones, hand carved with statues of angels, cherubim, and other heavenly figures adorning the cement. Then Jo's eyes widened as a sense of familiarity crept over her. She had seen this scene before! There were some differences, but . . .

Jo felt her breath catch in her throat with shock. Possum's old photographs that she had accidently dropped into the shark pool were almost exact duplicates. The difference was in the gravestones, which made the location more easy to identify.

With shaking hands, Jo carefully detached the sketch from the wall and made her way back to Glen. He and Reverend Morrison were standing facing the grave as the churchyard workers began filling in the hole.

Glen looked up and stopped talking in mid-sentence. Jo flapped her one good arm holding the sketch.

"Father Morrison, I found this picture down in the church basement. It's very much like a photograph that someone was murdered over. Do you know anything about it?"

Simon Morrison reached into his stark black cassock to find his glasses. Perching them on the end of his nose, he studied the sketch Jo had found.

"Why, yes. I recognize this location. It's right where Mr. Switec was buried. This row of trees was removed during my predecessor's time. That would be . . ." his myopic eyes glazed over in thought, "perhaps sixty or seventy years ago. But I remember hearing about these trees. Nasty, smelly things. Dripped some kind of sap that burned the skin. Anyway, when the cemetery was enlarged, the trees were cut down and removed. Wouldn't do to have them dripping all over the parishioners or their loved ones. But you can see for yourselves from the gravesites."

Father Morrison moved toward the tombstone marked Adams. It bordered the lot where Norman Switec had just been buried.

"Some of these lots were purchased by entire families for their loved ones when the members were relatively young. Always pays to plan ahead, you know."

Glen studied the picture. "So Norman Switec is buried close to the foot of where these trees were located?"

"So it would seem. Father Gephart, my predecessor in the parish, said the entire stumps were removed. Wouldn't do to have the wretched things sprouting up again after the fact."

Jo listened carefully. Her eyes went to the break in the thick vegetation, where the sea was barely visible.

"It's possible this location was originally part of one of the shoales and closer to the water," she muttered excitedly.

"I suppose so, but that would be a very long time ago. Hundreds of years, even." Father Morrison swatted at one of the large, black flies that buzzed around his face.

Glen Howard glanced up at Jo sharply. "Are you thinking what I'm thinking?"

"It could be that Cristabel saw Blackbeard and his men bury the treasure here on Roanoke Island. She wasn't clear about the location."

"Cristabel? I've heard that name before." Father Morrison's eyes trailed over the stones in the graveyard, to an older section in front of the side door of the church.

"Here. Is this who you are referring to?"

Glen and Jo followed in his footsteps. The stone was

white with age, small and rather squatty. Some of the letters were half-worn off, along with part of the inscription of "Dearest Mother."

Jo knelt down and ran her fingers lovingly over the stone. "She did come back at the end. After her husband died."

Glen looked at the grave. "Ironic. She was buried here so close to where she had been kidnapped."

"And Blackbeard must have buried the treasure here before sailing on to Ocracoke, where he was killed in a sea battle." Jo stood up and dusted off her hands.

"Father, we have a rather unusual request," Glen Howard began. "I'd like to see if Blackbeard's treasure really was buried under those poison trees."

"My son," Father Morrison said sadly, "if such was the case the treasure is gone. Long gone."

Glen looked blank. Jo finally queried gently, "What do you mean, Father?"

"Father Gephart kept extensive records in the church ledger. When the stumps were removed, well, it was forty or fifty years ago. Of course, nobody had any idea something was buried there. And . . . they used dynamite. A lot of dynamite."

"Dynamite?"

"Yes, my dear. No fancy explosive detonators like today. Sticks of dynamite. Blew gigantic holes in the ground when the tree stumps were removed. Had to bring in a ton of soil as fill dirt because the holes were so huge. That dynamite certainly did an excellent job and then some. Father Gephart said not a trace of anything remained for maybe ten or twenty feet down."

"I see, Father. And, perhaps it is for the best." Jo linked her one good arm through her husband's.

"The Lord gave and the Lord has taken away; blessed be the name of the Lord!" Father Morrison, intoned, trailing behind Jo and Glen back toward the main hall of the church.

Epilogue

All's well that ends well.
—Shakespeare

August, 2003

"**I** can't believe that the discovery of the *Queen Anne's Revenge* reached even the coast of Barbados!" Jo Howard leaned on the balcony railing of the luxurious beach house across from the lobby of the Palm Terrace Hotel. A little, green-colored lizard with protruding black eyes scurried over the beige-colored wall of the adjoining suite. Down below, two of the gardeners, in blue and white hotel uniforms, worked in the hot August sun pruning the breadfruit trees.

Jo read slowly from the Barbadean newspaper to her husband, Glen, who was mixing rum swizzlers at the elaborate tamarind bar in the sitting room of their twenty-room house.

"The artifacts from the ship will be on display in the Beaufort Museum temporarily. A more permanent home is being discussed by Mr. Glen Howard, a leader in the community and a sponsor of the *Queen Anne's Revenge* salvage project, underwritten by Scisearch. Blackbeard's flagship sank off of the Carolina coast at an undisclosed location.

"Mr. Howard has stated his intention of making a permanent museum home for the artifacts along with a replica of the *Queen Anne's Revenge* on Ocracoke Island, North Carolina, which was Blackbeard's base of operation back in the early seventeen-hundreds. However, Mr. Howard had added that these plans will have to be approved by the local citizens and town council before Scisearch will proceed."

Jo ran her eyes down the rest of the newspaper page. The article gave a summation of Blackbeard's career as a pirate, along with his friendship with Stede Bonnet, before their falling out while pirating together off the Carolina shoales. Details of Stede's life in Barbados, along with his unhappy marriage were touched upon. The article concluded with a brief mention about Mr. and Mrs. Howard currently residing on the island and wishing them a happy holiday.

Jo felt her husband's hand on her shoulder. His hands fumbled with her short, dark hair, which was slowly beginning to once more curl down her back.

"I'm glad you're letting the people of Ocracoke decide about the museum. And I'm glad that Cristabel's diary will have a permanent home at the Learned Owls bookstore. It was a good idea of Tara's, especially since she graduated and became my new manager. According to her, the diary may even help to bring in more business."

Glen's eyes traveled over his wife's head. In one of the poinciana trees a not-so-shy green monkey was peeking into the suite, eyeing the elaborate fruit basket on the dining room table.

"That's called delegating," Glen smiled. "And as for the museum, need I say that it will be up to the citizens of Ocracoke and that a bridge connecting the island to the mainland won't be far behind? But it will help the economy and more people will have jobs. New blood, new life. And Ocracoke, well, it is a beautiful island, as my wife pointed out to me many times in the past."

Jo smiled softly. "And will point out many times in the future. It is an ideal place to rest, relax . . ."

"And breathe healthy sea air." Glen Howard laughed.

"I've read the advertisements too. As a matter of fact, I've thought about writing a few."

The two dark heads came together, as Glen ran his finger lovingly down Jo's cheek.

The sound of beach pebbles striking the patio balcony was loud, disruptive, and impossible to ignore. Glen gave an exclamation of impatience, as Jo returned to her perch on the balcony railing and peered down.

"Turtle!" She exclaimed in delight. "It's great to see you again. And how is your mother?"

"She is very happy, Jo. And her fortune telling was right! A true seer of Barbados! You have returned to our island!"

Glen joined Jo at the balcony railing. Jo quickly introduced Turtle.

The boy eyed Glen up and down and observed him caressing Jo's hand.

"So is this the stinker of a husband, Jo?" he asked innocently.

Jo flushed red and glanced hopelessly at Glen. But her husband just grinned.

"Trust the words of children. And I was rather a stinker of a husband, I suppose."

"But the boy shouldn't just say . . ." Jo stopped in mid-sentence, staring at Turtle's back. It looked straighter, more aligned.

"Turtle!" Jo's voice was a half-croak. "Your back! It's straightened!"

The boy preened proudly. "Yes. I do not have to wear ugly tee-shirts anymore. And the children I play soccer with do not call me tortoise. Sometimes," he confided, "they even call me Tyrone!"

"But how? When?"

"After you leave, Jo, my mother receives a call from the hotel. It is helpful Octavia from the desk. She tells my mother the operation has been arranged and paid for here, at Queen Elizabeth Hospital, and the best doctor will be coming from the United States to take care of my back. It will no longer look hideous and deformed, and the children will no longer make fun of me."

"But is it true, Turtle?"

"It is just like Octavia says. Doctor comes, fixes back. And I . . . I am never so happy before!"

"But the doctor. And the hospital! Who paid for . . ."

Then suddenly Jo looked at Glen. He had been quietly studying the ceiling fan, avoiding her astonished gaze.

"Never mind, Turtle. I think I know!"

Turtle waved. "I must leave. Tourists want to go out on my jet ski. And they do not like to wait. Especially for bargain rate of just one hundred dollars. American! I am a great entrepreneur, am I not?"

Then Turtle vanished, sandals flapping, down the path past the Devon Rex cat, who now had a litter of kittens, and out toward the blazing white beach.

"So, stinker of a husband, you paid for the boy's surgery. After Octavia told you. And after what I said!"

"Yes, Octavia told me. And I told her to arrange everything. I said," and here Glen pressed his face to Jo's hair and murmured low in her ear, "I said I hoped we might be coming back soon. Together. And I wanted Turtle to be a special surprise for a very special someone, who I had lost but was trying so desperately to find again."

Jo turned full into his arms and moved away from the brilliant sun warming the balcony. "Let's go back to bed, my love."

"I don't think we're going to be doing much sleeping, though."

"And that," she muttered, "is exactly the way I want it!"

The late afternoon sun slithered past the window blinds and made speckled patterns across the parrot-colored rug and shadowed the two people seated on the sofa.

Jo's head rested lightly against her husband's shoulder, her eyes squeezed shut in happiness.

"Josephine," Glen murmured, his mouth planting tender kisses down the line of her throat, "I was just wondering . . ."

"Uh, what Glen?"

"Those divorce papers that I said I'd sign. What ever happened to them?"

Jo opened her eyes wide and looked at him with feigned innocence. "Divorce papers? What papers are those?"

9-04